Sealed with a Kiss

DIARY ♥F
A CRUSH

By Sarra Manning
Adorkable
Nobody's Girl
Guitar Girl
Let's Get Lost
Pretty Things
Fashionistas series

Diary of a Crush series
French Kiss
Kiss and Make Up
Sealed With a Kiss

Sealed with a Kiss

DIARY F
A CRUSH

SARRA
MANNING

atom

www.atombooks.net

ATOM

Written by Sarra Manning and based on
the *J17* column *Diary of a Crush*

First published in Great Britain in 2004 by Hodder Children's Books
This paperback edition published in 2013 by Atom

A CIP catalogue record for this book
is available from the British Library.

ISBN 978-0-349-00158-6

Printed and bound in Great Britain by
Clays Ltd, St Ives plc

Papers used by Atom are from well-managed forests
and other responsible sources.

MIX
Paper from
responsible sources
FSC® C104740

Atom
An imprint of
Little, Brown Book Group
100 Victoria Embankment
London EC4Y 0DY

An Hachette UK Company
www.hachette.co.uk

www.atombooks.net

Acknowledgements

Thanks to Ally Oliver, my editor at *J17*, who commissioned me to write the *Diary of a Crush* as a monthly column and her successor, Sophie Wilson, for continuing to commission me to write *Diary of a Crush*.

I would also like to thank Emily Thomas for giving me my first proper book deal after reading *Diary of a Crush*, my agent Karolina Sutton for working so hard and tirelessly on my behalf and Samantha Smith, Kate Agar and all at Atom for giving these books a shiny, new home.

Finally, I'd like to thank all the readers of *Diary of a Crush*. From the *J17* days, to the people who bought the books first time round, to you (yes YOU!) discovering Dylan and Edie for the first time. What a long, strange trip it's been.

Dedicated to the late, great, never out of date Gordon and Regina Shaw, who put up with me when I was a teenager.

Manchester – America – London
Edie's Diary Volume 3

I can't believe that my diary now has volumes! I'm, like, a twenty-first century Samuel Pepys or possibly someone less old, uncool, male and, y'know, *dead* who also kept a diary.

Anyway, my life up till now has been girl (that would be me), meets boy (that would be Dylan) and then fast forward through two years of torturous back and forth, kissing and fighting and all points in between. And now it's all different. Dylan and I have been back together for nearly a month and we've managed not to have a single argument. Weird. Carter (the king of evil ex-boyfriends) is still seething in the background but thankfully there have been no sightings of Veronique (his sister and the queen of evil ex-girlfriends).

And the other less-Dylan-y, but just as important parts of my life involve working in a café, being in a band with my friends, Poppy, Atsuko and Darby, and trying to decide what I want to be when I finally grow up.

12th September

Dylan and I haven't done it for two weeks. Having the parents back from their second honeymoon thing is kinda cramping my style.

There's, like, nowhere to go that doesn't involve secluded corners of parks or spending vast sums of money on a hotel room. And although the getting pelvic is fantastic, I kinda enjoy all the furtive kissing that doesn't lead anywhere.

Sex is strange. It's like this big secret that I have that no-one else knows about. Like this place that only Dylan and me have been to. Before the 'rents came home, he spent all his time here. And we'd just disappear under my covers, popping out now and then to load up with supplies from the fridge. It's not like we were doing it all the time, because we weren't, but the rest of the world just slipped away until all there was was Dylan and me. And what we used to be is nothing like what we've become.

When it's dark and the only light is coming from the muted television set in the corner of my bedroom, he talks in whispers about everything. His family and his dreams and what makes him frightened. Most of which I'm not going to put down here 'cause it's private – it's Dylan's story, not mine. But it made me understand why he is like he is, which is moody and difficult and messed up but still the sweetest boy you could ever hope to meet.

And did I mention the part where I fall in love with him a little bit more every day? It's a lot like drowning but the water feels so warm and wet against my skin that I don't really mind.

14th September

We had another band rehearsal tonight. We're starting to sound like a proper group. If proper groups sang songs about pink Converse All-Stars and had a lead singer who insisted on hula-hooping during the fast songs. Poppy is becoming more and more of a mentalist every day, which leads me to the part where me and Atsuko and Darby were just packing away our gear when Poppy suddenly dropped her bombshell. 'Oh by the way,' she announced casually. Way too casually. 'We're playing a gig next month. On Halloween actually.'

'What?!' we screamed in unison.

'What's the what?' she asked innocently. 'There's no point in rehearsing forever. We're ready for a paying audience.'

'But, but, but . . .' stammered Darby while Atsuko narrowed her eyes and began cursing under her breath in Japanese. That is, I think they were swear words, I couldn't be entirely sure.

Poppy began to twitch. 'Is that the time? Gotta go.' Then she practically ran out of the room though she'd never admit that she was too chicken to stay and face her band-mates' wrath.

'I'm so going to kill your sister,' I told Grace as we walked to the chippy later.

Grace didn't look too perturbed. 'She's just impulsive,' she said in her tiny voice. Since we got back from the festival, Grace and I have become mates. Well, I talk and she listens. I think the whole having-her-Highland-Spring-spiked-with-acid incident made her realise that she actually had to take part in life, instead of just observing it from the sidelines. Since then I've made a point of trying to drag her out of her shell. Because I'm all heart, in case you hadn't noticed.

As we reached the top of her road, my mobile started ringing. It was Dylan.

'Hey you,' I said softly.

'All my flatmates have disappeared off to Altrincham for an all-night rave,' Dylan drawled.

'And?' I prompted.

'Fancy a sleepover?'

'Cool! Shall I bring DVDs and ice cream?' I enquired.

'Just bring yourself and your toothbrush,' Dylan purred. 'And I'll provide the entertainment.'

Yay! I'm going to get seduced tonight. Go team Edie!

15th September
What I like about staying over at Dylan's:

1. He has a proper double bed, even though he chooses to encroach on my half of it.
2. He always wakes me up with a kiss and a cup of coffee.
3. The smoochies part of staying over gets better and better.
4. Even though they're a pikey student household, they have a far more expensive cable package than we do at home so we can watch Bollywood films till really late and make up the dialogue.
5. Dylan's there.

What I don't like about staying over at Dylan's:

1. Communal bathroom with no power shower, toilet seat always *up* and Carter barging in (the flimsy lock was no match for the arrogant way he flung the freaking door open without knocking) while I was cleaning my teeth.

Luckily I was clothed. 'Cause I learnt pretty quickly that you don't wander round in your underwear when your boyfriend lives with other boys.

I glared at Carter, but it was pretty hard to pull off when I had a mouthful of toothpaste, which was threatening to dribble down my chin.

'Oh, you stay over now, do you?' Carter enquired with a nasty smile. 'God, you've gone from shy virgin to experienced woman of the world in sixty seconds.'

I spat a big mouthful of foam into the basin and pointed at the door with my toothbrush. 'Get out!'

But Carter just stood there, grinning like the total, toxic cretin that he is. 'You know something, sweetheart?' he said in a low, confiding tone, leaning closer to me. 'You're not looking as cottony fresh as you used to. In fact, you seem a bit worn-in, a bit pounded, if you get my drift.'

I took a step back to get away from him and got banged in the butt by the edge of the sink. 'Firstly, ewww! And secondly, get the *hell* out!' I said furiously, but I kept my voice down because if Dylan knew that Carter had come into the bathroom while I was in there, let alone knew what he'd just said to me, it would have been like the Iraqi Conflict all over again. But with art boys.

I made another threatening gesture with the hand that was brandishing my toothbrush and with that stupid, inane chuckle of his, Carter finally got out.

It left me in a bad mood for the rest of the day.

19th September

Dylan'll be going back to university at the end of this week. That means no more smooching in the storeroom 'cause he's also starting back at his regular part-time job in Rhythm Records next door.

'It's a good excuse to have a party this weekend,'

6

Poppy pointed out as I bemoaned the disadvantages of not having a willing kiss-object at my beck and call.

'Well it would make a nice break from the chip fat in here and being in a band with a complete slave-driver who wants me to rehearse twenty-four seven,' I agreed.

'It's just over a month to go till our gig,' Poppy reminded me yet again. 'We have to be perfect. In a really cool, rock 'n' roll kind of way.'

I waved my hands in front of her face. 'Between mastering A flat diminished and the endless washing-up, my fingers are seizing up. I'm going to start charging you for my hand-cream supplies.'

'Stop being a drama queen and go and take this order to table five.'

I'm sure I'm developing calluses on the tips of my fingers from all that strumming action. Plus I have to have really short nails now and the polish just gets scraped off as soon as I apply it. This rock 'n' roll stuff is not in the least bit glamorous.

21st September
If I thought I could spend the next year waiting tables while waiting to be famous, The Mothership has other ideas. She's got this notion that I should spend my gap year doing something worthy (translation: *boring*) like working in the Third World or going trekking in the

Hindu Kush. What she really means is that she doesn't like me going out with Dylan. Not when I could be having a proper, committed relationship with the 'lovely Jake'.

'Carter was an evil, scheming rat,' I told her till I was blue in the face.

'Well he had charming manners,' my mum said mildly. 'While Dylan, well he's very glowery, isn't he?'

Jesus!

22nd September

I took the day off so I could spend some quality time with Dylan before he becomes re-immersed in doing art boy stuff.

We went to the Tate Modern in London and after we'd admired the Warhols we walked hand in hand by the Thames, which isn't a patch on the Manchester Ship Canal, quite frankly.

'I hate that summer's over,' I moaned as we sat down on a bench. 'There's absolutely nothing to look forward to.'

'Winter's good too,' said Dylan. 'We can stay in and I'll paint while you play the guitar and we'll be cosy even when it's all dark outside.'

And where was the fun in that? 'Yeah, but your central heating doesn't work,' I reminded him, thinking back to a party they'd thrown last winter when I'd had to keep my coat on for, like, the entire three hours I was there.

Dylan grinned and shook his head at me. 'You're such a princess.'

'My mum doesn't think so.' I rested my head against his shoulder because that's my head's preferred resting place these days. 'She thinks I should be travelling round Asia in my gap year. Like, I would ever go anywhere that doesn't have public lavatories. *Clean* public lavatories.'

'We could go somewhere next summer,' Dylan said but I thought he was trying to get me off the topic of public conveniences.

'Like where? Blackpool? Or, hey, maybe we could go back to Paris at a push.'

Dylan gave a start and I had to sit up. 'Oh! Yeah! We should go to America.'

'Dream on, D. It would cost a fortune.' I stood up and stretched lazily. 'But my limited funds will stretch to a couple of ice creams.'

'It wouldn't have to cost that much. I have some money in the bank from the guilt fund my dad left me when he walked out anyway,' Dylan continued, leaning forward and yanking me back down on the bench. 'If we went next summer we'd have a whole year to save up and we could hire a car and do a road trip. Road trip, Eeds!'

I still wasn't convinced. 'So you think we'll still be together then?' I asked him.

He touched my face lightly. 'You don't get rid

of me that easily.' He moved closer to me and brushed my mouth with his. 'Just think, we could go to New York, LA, San Francisco . . .' He nudged me with his elbow. 'You know you want to.'

He was right. I did. I wanted us to stay together and I wanted to do stuff with him. Exciting, adventurey stuff like going on a road trip in a cool car and going to places that I'd only seen in films. And shopping. A girl could do some serious shopping in the land of rampant consumerism.

'Well I have always wanted to go to New Orleans,' I admitted carefully. 'And Seattle, maybe Chicago, oooh! And we *so* have to go to Las Vegas! Oh God, we're going to do this, aren't we? We're going to do a road trip and I'm going to save all my tips and empty out my Marc Jacobs shoe savings account . . .'

Dylan jumped up so he could pull me to my feet, hoist me up and swing me round till I squealed because I was getting dizzy. 'Think of all those cheap motel rooms too! Double beds, no parents, no friends, no annoying flatmates.'

'Talking of which my parents have got a do tonight.'

Dylan smirked and leered at me at the same time, which was quite a feat. 'So that means . . .'

'An empty house. C'mon let's go and get the train home.'

23rd September

We decided to have the surprise 'Dylan leaving-the-café-and-not-before-time-because-he-was-the crappiest-short-order-cook-in-the-world, ever' party in a bar. I spend entirely too much time in the café as it is.

I blew my entire month's tips (but I'm going to start saving for Operation: Road Trip from tomorrow) on a wildly expensive, almost designer, floaty dress and was just twirling in front of the bathroom mirror so I could see the effect of optimum floatiness, when I heard Dylan ring the doorbell.

Dylan was wearing his most scruffy jeans (and that's saying something – I think his other jeans sneer at them and don't want to hang next to them in the wardrobe because they make them look bad) and a paint-splattered T-shirt. He looked at me in bewilderment.

'You look good but we're only going to the pub,' he spluttered as my mother glared at him.

'Well, I think Edith looks beautiful,' she began with a decidedly crisp edge to her voice.

I pulled Dylan doorwards. 'Don't wait up for me,' I hissed at her.

After much lying and tugging on his arm, I managed to get Dylan to the bar even though he was hell bent on holing up in the old man's pub at the top of my road and playing pool.

I think he began to twig that something was going

on when I practically had to have a full-blown hissy fit to get him on the bus into town. I'm actually pretty lousy at keeping secrets and so when Dylan started interrogating me within an inch of my tender, young life about where I was dragging him off to, I had to resort to silence. And staring stonily out of the window, while Dylan tried to cajole me into spilling. 'C'mon, Eeds,' he said in a voice all dark and treacly. 'You going to tell me what you're up to?'

When he resorted to tickling, which is so not funny especially as it makes me feel like I'm going to wet myself, I had to get up, climb over his legs and go and sit somewhere else until he promised to behave. I think he'd pretty much guessed by the time we got to the bar and he saw the sign that said, 'Closed for a private party', garnished with a handful of fancy balloons. He wagged a reproachful finger at me as he pulled open the door so Italian Tony could envelop him in a big, sweaty bear hug.

'You think we let you go without saying goodbye?' he bellowed in Dylan's ear and then Anna, our boss, was getting in on the act and kissing him.

'If you weren't leaving, I'd have had to sack you,' she laughed, as I pouted and wished she'd get her ex-boss hands off of my current boyfriend.

Poppy saw my mardy expression and rolled her eyes at me and I'd just taken a step towards her and the bottle of wine she was brandishing in my direction when Dylan snaked his arm round my waist and pulled me against him.

'I'm going to kill you for this,' he threatened but I was glad to see that he was smiling. 'You little minx.'

It was such a good night. There was cake (not made by Dylan, thank the Lord) and dancing and everyone that I loved was there. Nat, Darby, Atsuko, Poppy, the boys from Rhythm Records and Shona and Paul. And Dylan would catch my eye and look at me as if I was the most beautiful girl in the bar. Which I wasn't but it was very nice of him to think so. The whole party was turning into one of those perfect moments that you want to put in a box and only take out when you're feeling down. A memory that smelt like Poppy's rose perfume and sounded like Dylan *giggling* as he read all the rude messages on his card and looked like the tiny cascades of lights that sparkled off our glasses. I wanted it never to end. Any of it. But of course, it did – at just about the moment when I came out of the loos and started heading towards the bar and I was shoved out of the way by a girl with long, red hair who flung her arms round Dylan's neck and announced loudly, 'I'm back for the new term, honey. And I've decided to forgive you.'

It was Veronique.

I have to stop for a bit now while I wait for the feelings of rage, anger and wrath to shift down to more manageable levels.

23rd September (later)
I'm still very uncalm.

23rd September (even later)
Yeah! So where was I? Veronique! Back like a skanky apparition from beyond the grave.

To be fair, Dylan looked horrified when she suddenly tried to wrap herself around him like some poisonous trailing vine. He pushed her slowly but firmly off and said something to her that I was too far away to hear. Whatever it was, she didn't like it. She pursed her mouth, put her hands on her hips and tossed her stupid hair back and forth.

'Where did Cruella park her broomstick?' asked my gay best friend, Nat, as he poured some more wine into my glass.

I narrowed my eyes. 'I don't know,' I bit out. 'But I'm going to make sure she hops back on it.'

But Nat grabbed me by my arm before I could go over and do anything stupid, like hitting her, or screaming obscenities at the top of my voice.

'Nuh-huh, sweetie,' he cautioned me. 'You don't go into the ring until you're tagged.'

I had to watch her simpering at Dylan but whatever he was saying to her didn't seem to go down very well. She'd now progressed to some hardcore eye-rolling, while Dylan looked like he'd gone into 'try to reason with the idiot child' mode and then his face suddenly changed – when Dylan gets mad his face closes off. It's weird. Like all his features shut down, until all there is is this blank mask that you can't penetrate.

He was pretty much doing that now.

Then she started jabbing her finger into his chest and I had a brief flash of déjà vu to that scene where she tried to beat him up on our way to the festival.

'I can't just stand here!' I squawked at Nat who had a death grip on my shoulders. 'She's giving him a really hard ti—'

Just as I was trying to finish the sentence, I saw the curving arc made by Veronique's hand as she sent it crashing against Dylan's face.

'Fuck!' I wrenched myself out of Nat's hold and stormed over to Dylan, my feet skidding on the wet floor and almost knocking Shona flying.

'Edie!' I could dimly hear her calling to me but I didn't have time to stick around, I just wanted to see if Dylan was OK.

Veronique had gone back to poking his chest. 'It's not over until I bloody well say it is,' she was screaming at him as I tugged myself away from Shona and Nat who were both trying to grab on to whatever bit of me they could get hold of.

'Dylan!' Oh God, finally! I shunted Veronique out of the way with my entire body and flung myself at him. 'Are you all right? Did she hurt you?' Then I was clutching at him, running my hands up his chest so I could stroke his reddened cheek gently with the back of my hand.

'I give you a whole month to miss me and you and this bitch are *still* together?'

Dylan's face was still all tight and closed but he squeezed my hand.

I swivelled round and fixed Veronique with a glare. 'If you don't piss off right now, I'm going to—'

'Edie . . .' Dylan said warningly. 'Just leave it.'

Veronique put her hands on her hips and gave me a sweet smile. 'Oh, what are you going to do, dearie? Take away my TV privileges?'

I didn't actually know what I was going to do. The last time I saw Veronique she'd almost managed to scalp me but that kind of seemed like an irrelevant detail. She'd gatecrashed D's leaving do and hit him and she was evil and had to be stopped.

'Last time we had a fight, I pushed you into a pit full of poo,' I growled at her. 'You really don't want to stick round and find out what I do for an encore.' I sounded scary. Really scary. Possibly deranged too.

Veronique tried to smirk but gave it up as a bad job. 'You two losers deserve each other,' she snarled before disappearing in a cloud of sulphurous smoke. Except actually she used the door.

Dylan pretended everything was OK after that but it

so wasn't. Everyone kept asking him if he was all right and I think he was embarrassed that the cheek-smacking had happened in full view of all his friends who'd then witnessed his wimpy girlfriend see off his evil ex-girlfriend while he'd stood there.

So he did what boys do in those sorts of situations and got absolutely hammered.

Urgh! Anna drove us back to my place because Dylan couldn't find his keys and he threw up all over our garden path.

I was hoping that maybe it would rain in the night so my parents wouldn't find out. I managed to get inside and stagger to the kitchen with Dylan draped over me like a boy-shaped, beer-stinking blanket in the vain hope I could pour tons of black coffee down his throat and sober him up.

I was filling up the kettle while Dylan pressed himself against me and started licking my neck like an over-eager puppy when my dad came downstairs.

'Edith! What have we told you about curfews?' he started to say but was interrupted by Dylan leaning past me and puking up in the sink.

Then there was lots of shouting and Dettol. More shouting. Dylan slumping over the kitchen table. A bit more shouting. Dylan being banished from the house forever. And then more and more shouting.

And then some extra shouting just for luck.

You know, this is all Veronique's fault.

27th September

My mum is still not talking to me! It's not like *I* was drunk and then sick over every available surface. I've tried to explain what happened like a million times but she just keeps going on about how Dylan is a bad influence and then remembering that she's not speaking to me.

So I go out a lot. I go to work and then I go and see Dylan or I crash at Poppy's or Shona's (but mostly at Dylan's) and then she gets mad that I'm treating the house like a hotel. But if it was a hotel then I might get breakfast made for me and not have to do my own laundry. Also, I'd have Belgian chocolates put on my pillow every evening.

And Dylan's being weird and has been ever since Veronique-gate and I can't help but replay what happened the first time we started dating and how quickly it all descended into not dating. I couldn't bear it if that happened again but he's so hard to talk to sometimes.

We haven't really talked about him and Veronique. It's pretty obvious that she used to scream and beat him up at regular intervals (Shona's been a bit more forthcoming on the subject) and I think he sees it as a massive loss of face. Which it isn't. I'd be more worried if he used to scream and hit her back.

It's just I thought Dylan was over his intimacy issues (and why yes, I do sound like a really crap US Movie

Of The Week) but he's gone all closed-off and 'don't want to talk about it' again.

Just when everything had been getting so good.

29th September
Oh no! I've just had a text message from Dylan saying that we have to talk. I'm not getting happy feelings about this.

30th September
Forget what I said. 'Cause everything's different. In just the best and most beautiful of ways. Mostly. Dylan took me out last night to this little French restaurant and held my hand all the way through dinner. I'm not worried about Veronique any more 'cause instead of doing what I used to do, which was sulk and seethe about stuff, I just came right out with what was bothering me. Like, I was an actual mature person.

'We have to talk about Veronique,' I insisted as the waiter fussed and faffed about opening our bottle of wine. Dylan pulled a face and wound his napkin round his fingers, but tilted his head to indicate that I could continue, if I wanted. Which I *so* didn't, but had to.

'Right,' I started decisively. 'You had this relationship with her and I can deal with that but it seems like there was weird stuff going on that you don't want to talk about. Like, you're worried I'll think less of you or something. And I need you to know it won't happen. I mean, me thinking less of you.'

It was all a bit garbled and not making much sense. Dylan rubbed his hair and sighed. 'I can't talk about this stuff. I just can't. I screw up every relationship I have, you already know that.'

But I wasn't going to let him get away with self-defeatist crap like that. Not when we'd only just got back together.

I waved my fork warningly at him. 'God, don't be such a drama queen! You're not getting rid of me, Dylan. I'm here for the long haul so, hey, you'd better get used to it.'

And then it all spilled out, in this long, stream-of-consciousness purge. Dylan's mushroom crêpes went cold as he vented out all this stuff about how going out with Veronique had been this shame spiral that he couldn't drag his way out of. And that he'd been stuck in the middle of some emotionless void with a girl who spent most of the time telling him he was a waste of space and that no-one but her would ever want him.

'But you knew that wasn't true,' I protested. And I hated that there was a table between us because I wanted to gather Dylan up in my arms and keep him safe so no-one else could hurt him. 'I wanted you! I never stopped wanting you.'

He looked like a little boy as he fiddled with his napkin and wouldn't look me in the eye. Then he said in this choked voice that made my insides hurt: 'Yeah but the women in my life mostly tell me that I'm a worthless piece of crap.'

''Cept me,' I said because he had to know that.

Dylan looked up and his eyes were glistening and more green than I'd ever seen them, like the tears were just about to spill down his cheeks.

'Yeah, 'cept you.'

There was this long pause as we gazed at each other. Or I gazed and Dylan fidgeted. He'd torn his napkin to shreds and was now rifling through the little pile of torn up tissue-paper with his fingers.

Then all of a sudden Dylan looked up, took a deep breath and said, 'You've made me happier than I've ever been. Do you really think I'd let Veronique or anyone mess that up? God, I'm in love with you, Edie, how can you not know that?'

All of the bad stuff just seemed to melt away. It's not like I'm one of those sappy girls who are only validated by their boyfriends but Dylan's been this really important part of my life for over two years and this was the first time he's said he loved me. Well, actually no. He said he loved me before when we were split up but I think it was in the same way he loves Coco Pops. But now's he's *in* love with me, which just seems more passionate and like he'd die for me. Or at least give me the last chip off his plate without putting up too much of a fight about it.

Of course I had to say something snarky in reply. It was that, or start crying. 'I don't think I've ever made anyone happy before. Can you say responsibility?' I blurted out and Dylan almost spat his mouthful of green salad on to the tablecloth. Then he sniggered.

'See, anything you say or do Edie, seems kind of adorable these days.' He frowned. 'Which pretty much makes me your bitch.'

'If you were my bitch, then I think you'd actually be less with the brooding and more about buying me expensive presents and giving me backrubs and, oooooh!, getting up extra early so you could give me a lift into work and . . .'

'I'd quit now, while you still have a boyfriend, Eeds.'

It worked! Dylan wasn't broody or being all scary depressed any more. His lips were twitching and the corners of his eyes were crinkling up. Though in a very attractive way.

Then his knees nudged mine under the table and that was all it took to persuade me that we should go home and it would be no big deal to sneak Dylan in to my bedroom.

It would all have been fine and dandy if my mum hadn't decided to wake me really early so she could talk about my 'lifestyle choices'. Oh dear.

3rd October

I swear to God, out of me and my mother, I'm the grown-up.

I sat her down this morning, made her a strong cup of coffee and told her that Dylan and I were having a relationship and there was no need for her to be so bent out of shape about it.

'I appreciate that, Edie, but he's hurt you before and he'll hurt you again.' She said it with such finality. Like it was just this inevitable thing that would happen.

'He's changed and I've changed,' I protested. 'I'm less, well, less . . . less *crushy* this time. I'm more in control.' Because telling her that I'd made Dylan my total bitch was not going to go down very well.

But I might just as well have not bothered at all.

'Yes, well, I'll bear that in mind when you're crying as though your heart will break because he's proved himself to be completely unreliable. *Again!*'

Huh! That's so like my mum to throw my own words back at me like dirty laundry that she wants me to put in the washing machine myself.

'Look, it's different this time. We're like committed to each other.' I could actually feel my face turning blue with the effort of trying to explain this. She, on the other hand, was looking more and more pissy with every word that came out of my mouth.

'If by committed you mean that you're having sex with each other . . .'

Mum now looked like she'd just taken a slug of hydrochloric acid. The effort not to roll my eyes and huff nearly killed me. 'Yes,' I admitted unwillingly. 'I'm having sex but you don't have to worry because we're being really responsible and I've had a sexual health check and we're using contraception . . .'

Considering that there's been many an excruciating time when *she's* sat me down and jawed on in great and embarrassing detail about sex, casually dropping clitorises and IUDs into the conversation when I've been trying to eat my dinner, I have no idea why what happened next actually happened next.

One minute I was chattering away about my trip to the sex doctor and how Dylan and I had decided to carry on using condoms rather than me going on the pill, the next she'd made this weird hissing sound through her teeth and slammed the coffee mug down on the table so hard that it shattered, spilling Kenco decaf all over the pair of us.

'Mum?!' I shrieked, as I jumped up and ineffectually tried to shake the coffee stain off my *Manchester Roller Derby* T-shirt. 'What's the matter?'

'You are not to have sex! Not in this house, not with that boy,' she shouted, loud enough that they probably heard her up in the Pennines. 'I absolutely forbid it.'

That made me mad enough to forget that I'd decided to be all logical and reasonable.

'Fine! I'll just have sex with him in someone else's house then!'

'Oh no, you won't!'

'Oh yes, I will.'

The whole thing descended into a pantomime crossed with the shouty bits from the *EastEnders* omnibus. Until we decided that we weren't talking to each other again.

Our worst ever row in the history of all our previous worst ever rows ended when Mum suddenly stopped screaming and banging cooking utensils down really hard on the draining board and said in a tight voice, 'This just about does it.'

'Does what?' I screeched because once my volume knob is turned all the way up to eleven, it kind of stays there.

'I've been talking to your grandparents and we've decided you should spend your gap year with them.'

'But they live in Brighton!' I protested.

'Exactly,' snapped my mum. 'I've had it up to here with you, young lady.'

That was my cue to storm upstairs (in fact, it was probably more of a flounce, than a storm), pull down my suitcase from the top of the wardrobe and start stuffing random things in it. I wasn't exactly sure what I was doing, which is why I'm now camped out in Poppy's spare room with only odd socks and a lot of empty CD cases.

The girls came round after I did a four-way hysterical text thing in the cab over here. Atsuko reckons that my mum is having trouble cutting the umbilical cord 'cause I'm an only child. Whatever. I think she's going through the menopause or else she's inadvertently inhaled too many cleaning fluids in her time and it's all catching up with her.

7th October

I think Poppy and Grace's mum believes that I'm actually her daughter that she mislaid for eighteen years. Every time I make noises about moving home she says, 'No need to make a decision yet.' This is probably 'cause being a guest I don't give her any lip and always help with the washing-up.

I think Mum *did* think I was staying at Dylan's (which I thought about but realised that it would make a bad situation about a gazillion times worse – plus ick!, possible Carter encounters). She phoned today. Ostensibly to see if I had clean underwear but I'm sure it was to check up on me.

Instead, we had part forty-seven of The Row, which started just after she begged me to come home, then became 'You need to have a proper life plan for your gap year' to the familiar soundtrack of 'we don't want you sleeping with *that boy* in our house'. I tried to explain that I was saving money to go to America next year (not mentioning the Dylan factor in that plan) and once again pointed out that I could just as easily sleep with Dylan in someone else's house at which point my mum burst into tears and I slammed the phone down on her.

Jesus! Why is she being so strange about this? I'm polite, I'm helpful (well, most of the time I don't need to be reminded to put my mug in the dishwasher), I'm entirely funding my own gap year and road trip without asking them for a single penny and I'm having protected sex in a proper relationship with a boy I've known for over two years. Y'know, as teenage daughters go, they really don't come much better than me.

11th October
Life is all hissy and tense at the moment when it should be really good because there's Dylan and my job, which is pretty cool apart from the huge quantities of chip fat involved, and the band and Poppy. Instead, I feel like I'm walking about with a big, black storm cloud directly above my head.

It didn't help that there was another Carter incident this morning. I was reaching up to get a mug out of the cupboard, humming along to the radio and generally trying not to think any Mum-related thoughts and there he was.

He didn't say anything sneery, but came and stood right next to me, then reached across me for the peanut butter and let his hand brush against my breast. I could tell by the way his lips quirked that it wasn't an accident.

It also wasn't an accident when I picked up the kettle that I'd just boiled and splashed a tiny bit of very, very hot water on his evil, boob-groping hand.

'Ow! Hell! Ow!'

'Sorry,' I trilled and then I turned round and gave him my best wide-eyed innocent look and he scowled and stomped out of the kitchen. I pretty much rock sometimes.

So does D. Poor D. He doesn't know what to do to make the whole Mum angst situation better, other than crawl under a rock but he does try. The trying consists of asking me if I'm all right a lot and the buying of many bars of sugary confection because Dylan optimistically believes that when it comes to girls and their problems everything can be solved by large quantities of chocolate. Oh, but if only it was that easy.

Last night, I couldn't sleep and I was sitting on his windowsill reading but mostly staring out at the street, when he sat up in bed.

'Why are you still awake?' he asked groggily, rubbing his fists into his eyes.

'My head's buzzing,' I said softly. 'Go back to sleep.'

But Dylan made me get back into bed by the simple act of reaching over and yanking me into it and then pulling the duvet over me and curling me up in his arms.

'I hate that I'm not talking to her,' I said, as he tried to get me to rest my head on his chest and I resisted because Dylan's way too bony to make a comfortable leaning post. 'I've never had an argument like this one before.'

'All mothers are clinically insane. I think there's a law or something.'

'But I don't want to have left home!' I burst out. 'I'm too young and stupid to have left home and it's just too full-on.'

'Like you're all scared and small and the world is this big, vast thing that's gonna swallow you up and you're worried that no-one will even notice that you've gone?' Dylan had obviously been listening to too much Radiohead but he had a point.

'You'd notice if I wasn't here, wouldn't you?' I asked and I wasn't really joking. My voice sounded tinny and flat and Dylan hugged me harder.

'You wouldn't get to be not here because I'd notice way before that,' he said firmly, his breath tickling my ear.

And then he stroked my hair very slowly and didn't stop until he knew I was asleep.

14th October
Ha! Carter's moved out. They came back from classes today to find that he'd done a flit taking the big telly

with him and owing a month's rent. Somehow I can't find it in my heart to care. *So* over him cornering me outside Dylan's room when I'm staying the night and making the most obscene remarks. I mean, really rude. So rude, that I didn't dare tell Dylan because he'd have gone ballistic. Still, don't have to worry about Carter any more.

Boys are very unstressy when it comes to stuff that isn't girl-related. I'd have been all bothered about having to sort out a new flatmate but if Simon, Paul and D became any more laidback they'd fall over.

It's just as well that my toothbrush is practically a permanent feature in their bathroom (Mrs Poppy doesn't really mind, other than making me let her know where I'm sleeping so she doesn't stay up worrying that I'm lying dead by the side of the road) because otherwise I wouldn't get to see Dylan at all. What with him doing the art boy thing and me doing the waitress thing and Poppy making us rehearse every evening, crashing out in his bed is about the only quality time we get together.

15th October
Dylan popped in for lunch today.

'I'll have a cheeseburger with all the trimmings, a full-fat Coke and the biggest portion of chips you do,' he said by way of greeting when I looked up from the espresso machine.

'And hello to you too,' I said distractedly, as I put the lid on a cappuccino for the harassed-looking suit who was giving Dylan the evil-eye for taking my attention away from the serving of his hot beverage. I've got pretty good at multitasking. 'Thank you, see you soon.'

Dylan just winked at me. 'If you get my lunch ready in super quick time, I'll make it worth your while.'

'Oh yeah, you're going to leave me a tip, are you?' Which would like be a first.

Dylan rested his elbows on the counter and curled his tongue behind his front teeth. 'I was thinking more of ravishing you in the storeroom, if you fancy it.' Sometimes he was too bloody cute for his own good.

'And they said romance was dead. Hello . . . can I help you?'

I continued making googly eyes at Dylan who was giving me a slow once-over in a way that wasn't entirely appropriate for lunchtime, and not paying much attention to whoever it was who'd come up to the counter when I heard a voice say:

'Do I know you from somewhere? You look terribly familiar.'

I recognised that voice! 'Dad! What are you doing here?'

He was standing there, clutching his briefcase and looking terribly pleased with himself.

'I heard a rumour that my daughter was actually still

on this plane of existence so I thought I'd see if it was true.'

Dylan had straightened up from trying to look down my shirt and was shifting nervously from side to side as my dad threw him an appraising look.

'And I know I've seen you somewhere before too,' Dad said mildly, which is never good.

Dylan tried to bundle his bag and his sketchbook and his wallet under his arm so he could stick out his hand in greeting and ended up dropping everything on the floor.

'Hello sir. Yes, I'm Dylan,' he mumbled as he bent down to pick his stuff up.

'Ah! That's where I know you from. Last time I saw you, you were throwing up in my kitchen sink.'

The two most important men in my life were holding up my lunch queue and it felt like matter and anti-matter trying to collide. I had no choice but to introduce them formally.

'Dad, this is Dylan, please behave. Dylan this is my father who I've inherited my sarcasm from. Feel free to ignore him.'

Then they shook hands and the earth managed to stay on its axis. Even when my dad spotted an empty table and gestured at Dylan, 'Shall we?'

Dylan looked like he'd just been given two weeks to live and shuffled unwillingly after my paternal signifier. Anna went over to take Dad's order and I hid behind the specials board to try and suss out what was going on and whether I needed to rush out and buy a bullet-proof vest.

Dad was being cooler than ice-cubes. He's like a master tactician. When he's like that with me, not saying much but giving me encouraging nods and little smiles, I often find myself confessing to all sorts of crimes, which used to result in being grounded and having my allowance stopped. Dylan was made of sterner stuff. Or moodier stuff, at least. He was ripping his napkin into little pieces (which is his favourite nervous habit) and refusing to maintain eye contact. Every now and again he'd open his mouth so I guess he was talking. He can be pretty fluent in monosyllablese when he wants to be.

My social anthropology was interrupted by some inconsiderate people who wanted to order drinks and I was so busy for the next half hour that it wasn't until Anna told me I could take my break that I realised that Dad and Dylan were still sitting there.

Italian Tony gave me a plate with my usual lunch on it of a jacket potato with chicken and tomato on the side, absolutely, positively not touching each other, and I slowly walked over to them.

'. . . so then I'm probably going to do a Masters and hopefully teach at the same time,' Dylan was saying, leaning back in the booth. 'That way I'll still get to work on my own stuff but I'll be able to earn some money.'

'That's sensible,' Dad nodded. 'Though it still seems to be a good time to be a YBA.'

'A YB what?' I asked, sitting down next to Dylan.

'A young British artist,' they answered in unison and I began to wonder whether I'd walked onto the set of *The Twilight Zone*.

'Like Tracey Emin or Jake and Dinos Chapman,' Dylan added.

I glared at my father who merely raised his eyebrows at me. 'Oh my God! You're like something out of Jane Austen. You've been asking Dylan about his prospects, haven't you?' I demanded angrily. 'Have you got to the part where you ask him whether his intentions are honourable?'

'Oh we covered that bit quite early on,' Dylan assured me. 'Relax, Edie, it's all good.'

'You can't trust him,' I said, stabbing at the jacket potato with my fork. 'He's sneaky.'

'Thank you, young lady.' Dad was smiling the smile of someone who wished they still had the power to withhold my TV privileges. 'I am sitting right here.'

'Yeah and I'd like to know why.' I prodded my jacket potato around a bit more before pushing my plate away.

'Your mother's been very upset,' Dad began, and I sighed heavily while Dylan gave me a warning nudge with his elbow.

'I know that she's being a little unyielding,' (I snorted at this), 'but she's having trouble letting go.'

Dad's voice was very gentle but there was a slight bite to his words, which stopped me from bursting forth with a rant about how utterly pissed off I was with her whole unyieldy routine.

To cut a long story a little bit shorter, Dad thinks it would be a good idea if Dylan came round for Sunday lunch, as every time they've met up till now, he's either been drunk, trying to do rude things to me or scruffily dressed. I can't really say that the inclusion of a side of roast beef and some Yorkshire puddings is going to help matters but apparently that goes to show how little I know.

20th October

Dylan's started freaking out about going to lunch tomorrow. Really freaking out.

'I don't do parents, Eeds. I've barely got one of them, let alone having your two on my case,' was his cheery greeting when I popped back to his on the way home.

His room looked like it had been attacked by a savage band of clothes-eating demons..

'Hey, noted and what's with all the clothes?' I said, clearing a tiny patch of duvet free of jeans so I could sit down.

'I haven't got a thing to wear,' Dylan wailed, clutching at his hair and then sending me a death stare when I giggled. 'It's not funny!'

'You know that you actually turned into a girl when you said that?' I giggled again and then gave up because he'd obviously buried his sense of humour under the pile of T-shirts on the floor.

We leafed through his clothes and couldn't find anything suitable to quell my mother's fears about him.

I love Dylan and I'm used to his quirky dress sense but it's not parentally friendly. I held up a particularly hideous shirt, which featured pale blue ruffles cascading down the front, that I'd always wanted to burn.

'What the hell were you thinking, D, when you bought this? It looks like a bingo caller died in it.'

Dylan snatched the shirt out of my hands. 'Really not helping,' he growled.

In the end, I went to find Paul and begged for the loan of a Fred Perry shirt and a pair of trousers, which his mum had bought him for Christmas and had been stashed at the bottom of his wardrobe ever since. I threw them at Dylan.

'OK, look, you can wear these and then we'll never, ever talk about it,' I said sternly.

Once he'd changed, Dylan nearly refused to let me see his makeover but I barged through the door and gawped at the transformation. Dylan looked, well, *normal* and UnDylan-y. He also looked like he was uncomfortable in his own skin, which was an entirely new vibe for him. He kept pulling at the shirt and trying to smooth his hair back while he stared stonily at his reflection in the mirror.

'I look like I'm going to a fancy dress party as a bloody townie,' he finally spat. 'God, I wouldn't do this for anyone but you.'

Then I realised something important. That this wasn't about what Dylan wore. It was the very fact that Dylan existed that was bugging my mum. 'I don't want you to,' I exclaimed. 'I don't care if you have weird dress sense and she doesn't either. Not really.'

Dylan turned and looked at me with a quizzical expression, even as he started yanking the shirt off so violently that buttons pinged into the four corners of the room. 'Sometimes, Eeds, you need to come with subtitles.'

'It's you that she's bothered about because we're together and she'd have ended up being bothered about Carter if we'd got more serious. So, it really isn't what you wear, though I'm never going out in public with you if you wear that bingo-caller's shirt.'

Dylan shrugged and all the muscles in his chest shifted in the most delightful way. I swallowed hard. Because I've seen Dylan without a top quite a lot, like, really a lot. But sometimes it's like I'm seeing all that olivey skin for the first time and it gets to me all over again. And he hadn't kissed me once since I got there. Plus, was it just me or had the room suddenly got very warm? Dylan's eyes locked into mine and I realised it wasn't just me.

'So she automatically hates me because I'm taking away her little girl,' he practically purred and started prowling towards me. It was all very predatory and guh-making.

'Yeah, I think it's because I'm an only child and they had me quite late. Makes her extra-squicky about boyfriends, y'know?'

I couldn't decide what to do with my body, which seemed to have a pretty good idea itself and was straining towards Dylan who was still doing a good impersonation of a panther. 'Sometimes I actually feel lucky that my dad walked out on me years ago and my mum's too messed up to ever be bothered about what I'm getting up to.' He paused. Looked me up and down and then pounced on me. 'Or who I'm getting up to!'

'Don't say that!' I squealed as I landed on the bed, quickly followed by Dylan launching himself at me. 'I'm sure your mum does care about you.'

But then Dylan cupped my face and there was kissing. Languid, long kissing that left me breathless and giddy and mothers and fashion decisions didn't seem that important.

22nd October

Poppy is working my very last nerve. We're rehearsing every night for four hours until Halloween. Which is not only costing a fortune in renting out the rehearsal room but cuts into my Dylan time, my down time and just about every other time you could mention.

Nothing else to report really. Dylan reckons he has the whole Sunday lunch sitch 'under control', to which I say a big 'yeah, right!'

Also, this new boy is moving into the flat with Dylan and the others. He's called Julie. No, he's not. But he has a sort-of girl's name that begins with J that I can't remember and he's in a band called The Sweet Janes and Dylan knows him 'cause he comes in Rhythm to put up flyers.

I've never seen his band but when I told the others they got really excited. Even Poppy! In fact, Poppy was worse than Atsuko and Darby and she doesn't normally get that into boys.

'So, it's definitely the singer from The Sweet Janes?' she suddenly said mid-song at last night's rehearsal.

'I s'pose.' I was too busy trying to remember the bridge to the chorus. 'D knows more than I do.'

'You're no help,' she said between gritted teeth. 'He's gonna be living with your boyfriend.'

I so wished I could remember his name but I contented myself by tormenting Poppy with a constant refrain of, 'You fancy him! You fancy the new flatmate with the girl's name. You love him! You want to kiss him!' And then she hit me really hard . . . so I stopped.

24th October

The day of the Sunday lunch. I feel like I'm going off to a UN peace summit or something. And why did I agree to let Dylan wear what he normally wears? I should have forgotten all that crap about Mum hating him just because he was doing me and insisted on outfit veto rights.

24th October (later)

Dylan is a god. There can be no other explanation. There I was, thinking he was a not-so-run-of-the-mill boy with slightly dubious dress sense, good with his hands and his mouth and a paintbrush and easel, and actually that was all an act. Because I think he must have drifted down from somewhere where they make gods after the miracles he performed over Sunday lunch.

First of all, he turns up wearing a very modified version of his usual geek chic. A pair of grey Dickies trousers that were actually held up by a belt instead of half-falling down, a black shirt that didn't have anything rude painted on it or any buttons missing. God bless him, he'd even shaved and tried to brush his hair.

And did I mention that he had a huge bunch of flowers clutched in his hand?

I actually felt a bit tearful because even after feeling so weird about his own absent parents, he was going to all this trouble to ease *my* parents' fears.

'I love you,' I mumbled and then flung my arms round his neck. 'I really, really love you.'

I could feel his smile against my cheek. 'I am pretty damn loveable.'

I gently disentangled myself from him. 'Yeah, and modest too. But, hey, joking aside, thank you and you know exactly what I'm talking about.'

And from the moment he thrust the bunch of gerberas at a rather taken-aback Mothership, I knew we'd probably get out of the lunch alive.

It was very awkward to start off with. Mum was talking too fast in this really high-pitched voice and not looking Dylan in the eye and Dad would say, 'Dear?' and then they'd go into the kitchen for two minutes, leaving Dylan to pull horrified faces at me.

We sat down to eat and for a while it was OK. Mum had catered for a football team and all the 'Why yes, I would like some mangetouts' and 'Gravy anyone?' took up some time. Not enough time though.

Despite the civilised clink of cutlery and our best china and the posh veg, it was like a bloodbath. Poor Dylan got interrogated like something out of the Spanish Inquisition. How many A-levels did he have? Had he run up huge student loans? What did his father do for a living? Wouldn't it make financial sense for him to live with his mother?

Dylan's shoulders were sinking lower and lower, even though I kept squeezing his hand under the table, and I opened my mouth to tell my mum to back the hell off when Dylan suddenly put down his knife and fork and said, 'Look, my dad walked out when I was eleven and my mum suffers from depression. I don't really have proper parents and it's hard for me to understand where you're coming from.'

That shut Mum up. She opened her mouth, thought better of it and closed it again. Instead she took a huge gulp of her Chardonnay.

I gave Dylan's thigh a warning pinch but he put his hand over mine and continued. 'I'm not trying to be rude, Mrs Wheeler. I know that I haven't always been good to Edie in the past. I wish I could change that but I can't. And you're right to be suspicious of me but I would never do anything to hurt her. I love her and I just want to make her happy.'

There was this long silence and I looked at my plate and the gravy that was going cold and congealing. I felt slightly sick.

I looked up and Mum was taking another glug of her wine and – I looked extra closely to be sure – there was a little tear trickling down her cheek.

Then Dylan picked up his knife and fork and began cutting up a roast potato like everything was normal.

Of course, my mum started crying and that made me start crying. Dad disappeared into the kitchen on the flimsy excuse that he wanted to load the dishwasher and took Dylan with him.

'I can't believe you were so rude to him!' I turned on her the minute we were alone. 'How could you ask him all those questions about his family and stuff? How do you think that made him feel?'

Mum just cried harder and it was horrible. Mums aren't meant to cry. I'd only ever seen her cry once before when my great-grandma died and although I was absolutely furious with her, I got up and went over to her.

'Mum, please stop crying,' I begged and patted her gently on the shoulder. As soon as I touched her, I was enveloped in her arms and she pulled me down so I was half-sitting in her lap.

'Hey! I'm not five any more,' I spluttered. 'I'll break your legs.'

We ended up on the sofa with my head in her lap and some serious head-stroking going on.

Then I embarked on this big speech about how I was eighteen and had to make my own decisions and I was not, repeat NOT going to spend my gap year with the grand 'rents. And that she had to manage to at least be civil to Dylan.

'Sometimes being a parent is hard, sweetie,' she said after I'd finished being all assertive. 'It's not like you came with an instruction manual. When you were born, you were this tiny little thing and I loved you so much. I knew I'd do anything to protect you and keep you safe. And that feeling doesn't go away just because you've got a boyfriend and a weekly wage.'

'I kinda realise that, Mum. But Dylan . . . he's really special.'

I looked up at Mum who then had the audacity to wink at me. 'How long do you think he rehearsed that speech for?' she demanded with a naughty smile that must have been a trick of the light.

'Still made you cry though, didn't it?' I tried to wriggle upright but she wasn't having it.

'You being all grown-up and striking out makes me feel slightly like a spare part. That you don't need me any more,' she admitted slowly. 'And it makes me feel old.'

This time I did scramble up so I could hug her. Hugging her is like coming home. It's utterly familiar; the feel of her in my arms, her hair tickling my cheek, the smell of Chanel No 5 and something that's particularly *her*.

'I'll always need you,' I muttered. 'But, like, not in the same way as before. I hate you not speaking to me and being angry with me so can we please just make up?'

And that was that. Though I'm still not sure that I want to move back home even though I can't keep staying at Poppy's and Mum would really bust a move if I shacked up with Dylan.

When I mentioned that it would be a really positive

step for our new understanding if she calmed down about me sleeping with him, she just did that selective memory thing that mothers are so good at.

By the time Dylan and Dad had re-emerged (Dylan later told me he'd had to nod and smile politely while he got a rundown on the many and varied problems Dad was having with his computer's operating system) Mum and I were having another glass of wine and arranging a mother/daughter bonding spa weekend.

Dylan helped her make coffee and I think he must have been pretty devastating in his charm offensive because she was all pink-faced and smiley and 'Oh, Dylan!' for the rest of the afternoon.

Thank God, it's over!

26th October

I've decided to stop worrying about family and worry instead about our impending debut gig. For about one minute last week, we were actually sounding good but now, despite the nightly rehearsals, we suck like a gaping chest wound.

Poppy who of course knows all her guitar parts and never forgets chords, and even knows what barre chords are, deals with the problem by yelling at us. We yell back. Then we sound even worse because we're too busy being mad at each other to concentrate on playing properly.

I keep hoping that a meteor will crash on the pub

where we're playing so the gig gets cancelled. Especially after Poppy and I had a blazing domestic yesterday and she told me that she'd only let me join the band because I had good hair. The good hair comment kind of sidetracked me for a second and then I went back to wanting to kill her. But I can't because I'm living in her house and I think it would really piss her mum off.

30th October

I feel like I haven't seen Dylan in days. We're rehearsing until eleven every night but we still sound like a bunch of amateurs. When we get home, Poppy follows me upstairs and stands over me and forces me to practise some more because I can't seem to remember any of our songs.

'How does it go again?' I have to ask her after about ten seconds because the remembering stuff bit of my brain seems to have short-circuited. Then she makes this noise that's somewhere between a growl and a scream that no human being should be able to make and slams the door, leaving me to not sleep because no girl has ever been under this kind of pressure. This time tomorrow night we'll be on stage! At least I found something to wear today. I'll be making my live debut in a black-and-pink American-diner, waitress uniform thingy, which looks tame compared to Poppy who describes her stage outfit as 'white trash prom queen'.

Ooooh! And we have stage names. I'm Edie Evil, Poppy is Supreme Dictator Bitch (actually she's Miss Pop Tart but I prefer the name I've given her), Darby is Dame Darby Dustbunny and Atsuko refuses to answer to anything other than Susie Samurai.

Actually, I guess I am a little bit excited . . .

31st October

I'm a bona fide guitar goddess! I'm going to have cards printed up and everything.

We rocked! Nobody even noticed that we hit a few bum notes and that Darby spilt a pint of beer all over me because we were too busy jumping up and down and screeching out the words in cheesy American accents. Poppy was just . . . She was awesome. She carried the three of us and just the way she moved, the way she sounded, I wanted to be her.

I mean, basically we're Poppy's backing band, it is The Poppy Show but she does it so well and so passionately that when we were on stage and I could see how she came alive, how she *glowed*, I got why she'd been so mad at us for not taking the band thing seriously. I know that five years from now I'll be interviewed by a film crew from MTV who are doing a special on Poppy and I won't feel any resentment that she's this cool famous icon, because she let me come along for some of the ride. I'm not entirely sure that she'll be so forgiving.

'This is Edie Evil. She ain't too good at playing the guitar but she looks mighty purty,' was how she introduced me, much to the audience's amusement.

Most of the crowd were our friends anyway who'd good-naturedly agreed to fork out a fiver for the privilege of seeing us behave in much the same way as we do on a night out. And being on stage, being part of something and having people watch me, *me!*, made me feel sexy and special and all those other things that I never normally feel.

When we got off stage Dylan was waiting for me. I was on such a high that I threw my arms round him and started kissing him passionately while the next band were trying to set up their equipment.

'I'm going to have to get a T-shirt printed up that says, "I'm with the band",' he said when we'd finally come up for air and were sitting at the bar with the others.

'Hmmm, we should definitely have T-shirts,' decided Poppy who was so over-excited that I thought she was going to implode. 'And maybe we could have umbrellas too. Or hairslides. I mean, T-shirts are so boring.'

It was very odd. Strangers kept coming up to us and asking when we were playing again and if we had a CD out. I felt slightly outside of myself but in a good way. Dylan had his arm round me and I watched Poppy hugging Grace, and Atsuko and Darby eyeing up some blokes and Paul and Shona waving at us from the other side of the club and I felt like I really belonged. Like I was part of this family that had nothing to do with my other family.

2nd November

I met the famous new flatmate when he moved in today. Name's Jesse and I can see why my fellow band-mates all go into a sugar coma when he comes up in conversation.

He looks like the result of a cloning experiment between Ryan Gosling and Kurt Cobain. He has this thatch of bleached blond hair, blue eyes the colour of Dylan's faded denim jacket, a smattering of freckles across the bridge of his cute little nose and to offset the pretty he has a filthy grin with, as I found out about five minutes later, a matching sense of humour. If my heart weren't already taken, I'd have fallen head over heels in lust with him.

As it was, I bowled into their lounge, threw the bag of salt and vinegar crisps that Dylan had asked me to get in the general direction of him and then stood there with my mouth hanging open when I caught sight of Jesse sprawled out on the sofa.

'This is Edie, Dylan's bird,' Simon drawled from the doorway. 'Get used to her, learn to love her, she practically lives here. Edie, you're starting to drool.'

I promptly put a stop to the slack jawing and

whirled round to give Simon the evil eye. 'I am not Dylan's *bird*. Thank you very much.'

'Bird, significant other, bitch, whatever, pleased to meet you,' Jesse said in this bewitching Irish brogue. I think I might have whimpered.

Dylan gave me an exasperated look and I felt a bit guilty. 'I bought you crisps,' I said to remind him of what a devoted girlfriend I was. He looked unimpressed.

'My friend Poppy really fancies you,' I blurted out, more for something to say and to stop Dylan giving me wounded glances.

Jesse sat forward. 'Is she cute?'

'She's super cute and she's really cool. We're in this band called Mellowstar and she sings and plays guitar. You'll have to meet her.'

'I love girls who rock,' Jesse beamed and then he took a swig of his Coke and let out a gigantic burp. 'Better out than in.'

And I decided that yes, he was drop dead beautiful but he had the manners of a pig and Dylan was actually way more gorgeous so I plonked myself down on his lap and gave him a sloppy kiss on the cheek, despite the rather rude comments from his housemates at such unwarranted public displays of affection.

5th November
Dylan is knee-deep in art stuff. His first big college show is coming up and he's way more interested in his

interactive *Star Wars* sculpture (just don't ask) than in interacting with me. I had to go to Atsuko's Bonfire Night shindig with Nat because Dylan was too busy making a huge vat of papier mâché.

Having said that, his flat has become the number one destination for all my friends who are hoping to get a glimpse of Jesse wandering around in his boxer shorts. A sight I've been witness to and hmmm, nice, but though I appreciate him on an aesthetic level, nothing compares to Dylan holding my hand as we wait for a bus or the way his face lights up when he sees me.

I even caught Shona ogling Jesse this morning. Her and Paul stumbled downstairs and she sent him out to the corner shop for some milk, by which time Jesse had wandered into the kitchen in a pair of jeans and she just stood there like one o'clock half struck.

But the thing about Jesse is that he's like this over-exuberant puppy. Even though all the girls they know are panting after him, it would be impossible for the boys to get pissy about it. Half the time Jesse is oblivious, though I don't understand why – has he never looked at himself in a mirror? – and the rest of the time he's making rude jokes about how he's gasping for a shag.

(Though if Poppy ever finds out that I told him about her crush on him, they'll be finding various parts of my body for months.)

11th November

It was very quiet in the café today. By the time the lunchtime rush was over, the place was deserted. Poppy and I re-filled all the ketchup doodads and were keeping an eye on a bunch of horrid, spotty boys in tracksuits who kept throwing sugar cubes at each other and were *so* bunking off when Jesse walked in.

'Hey Edie! How are you doing, sweetheart?' He came right behind the counter to peck me on the cheek while Poppy stared at him for a second and then turned away and pretended that the specials blackboard was totally rocking her world. It would have been really convincing too if she hadn't gone bright red.

'Jesse, you haven't met my best friend, Poppy, have you?' I said demurely. 'The one who's in the band with me.'

Jesse peered at the back of Poppy's head, which was practically the same shade of platinum blonde as his. God, they were made for each other! He sidled closer and then stood looking at her.

'What the hell are you staring at?' Poppy demanded and my heart sank. Her relationship philosophy could be loosely described as 'all boys are selfish gits who are good for nothing but a quick fling as long as they pay for dinner first'. There was a bad break-up with this guy she was in a band with before I met her, which she'll never, ever talk about.

'You,' Jesse said jovially, completely not put off by how rude Poppy was acting. 'Edie said you were cute, but . . .'

'Have you been talking about me?' Ick! She was using her scary serial-killer voice. I hoped that Italian Tony had cleared away all the big knives from the kitchen.

'I might have mentioned you in passing,' I said casually and then clocked the young tearaways going for the mayonnaise bowls. 'Don't even think about it if you like having kneecaps,' I shouted at them.

'Yeah, she said you fancied me,' Jesse added, not bothering to disguise the way he was looking at Poppy's boobs.

'I so did not!'

'I'm going to kill you!'

'So, do you wanna go out then?' Jesse was blithely unaware that I was this close to becoming human remains.

'Why should I go out with you?' Poppy asked flatly and I made a mental note to take her to one side and give her a few pointers on how to talk to boys.

Jesse, though, was gazing at her with what seemed to be adoration.

'Because I have a weakness for really bitchy girls and I'm a fantastic shag,' he said after a moment's deliberation.

Poppy then looked in the direction of Jesse's crotch

and raised her eyebrows as if to suggest that she was very sceptical about that claim.

'OK, you talked me round,' she sighed. 'I'll let you have a couple of hours of my time. Now stop staring at my tits before I clock you one.'

Jesse let out a long breath. 'You're like my perfect woman. I'm going to take you out and treat you like a little princess,' he promised.

And for one moment, Poppy shot him this blinding smile, which I think made Jesse fall in love with her on the spot. Then she screwed up her features into a sour expression again. 'Edie's our little princess, there might be copyright problems. Probably best if you treat me like the goddess that I am.'

Jesse doesn't stand a chance.

15th November

Dylan is still missing in action. He came into the café today and I was just about to go on a break so we could snog or at least have a conversation but he just ruffled my hair and said, 'Can't stop, just thought I'd say hi,' and disappeared, stuffing a cheese roll into his gob en route.

18th November

Poppy has her hot date with Jesse tonight. She was unusually flustered as she discarded one spangly dress and vintage T-shirt after another while Grace and I sat on her bed and said helpful stuff like, 'It's a bit low cut for a first date, you should definitely wear it' and 'The green one says slutty-but-shy. Not quite sure if you can pull that off, but, hey, Jesse might!' That was just before she ordered us out with much swearing and threats to dismember our corpses and dump them in the canal.

Jesse has forked out for two tickets to see Bon Iver and then maybe a drink afterwards if Jesse hasn't contravened any of Poppy's rules for acceptable first date behaviour. She has a very low tolerance threshold where boys are concerned. Or that's what she'd like us to believe. Really, she's so busy being kickass most of the time that it's hard for her to calm down and take time to get to know people. If we hadn't started hanging out through work, I wonder if she'd ever have had the patience to see beyond my slightly ditzy (though charming) exterior and become friends with me.

Then Grace and I went to the cinema. I haven't had a chance to spend much time with her lately but the dormouse attitude seems to be disappearing fast. In fact, I can't shut her up. And she's funny! Who knew?

The film we saw was pretty crappy but she spent most of it whispering sarcastic comments in my ear and making me spit out bits of popcorn.

As we were coming out of the multiplex we bumped into this boy I vaguely recognised from Rhythm

Records. He came up to us, opened and shut his mouth a couple of times, muttered something that might have been 'Hello' at Grace and then tripped over his feet in an effort to get away.

'What was all that about?' I asked Grace but she was blushing in exactly the same way that Poppy had when she'd met Jesse, and falling over her own feet.

I nudged her with my arm. 'He was sort of cute in a tousled, clothes-too-big-for-him way, but we could work on that,' I said casually. 'Where do you know him from?'

'Edie! Stop it!' Grace yelped and refused to talk to me for at least five minutes.

If I managed to set up both Poppy *and* Grace in the same month, then my own romance karma levels would go through the roof. Maybe Dylan might actually spend some time in the same room as me. Stranger things have happened.

30th November
Had a big, bad gloom today. Realised that I've been staying at Poppy's for nearly two months and it can't last forever. So I can either a) move back home with Mum and her variable mood swings b) move in with Dylan, the absentee boyfriend or c) use up all my wages and try to find somewhere to rent.

Talking of Dylan I was just having an extremely sarcastic rant at him inside my head as I locked up the café, when I realised he was standing in the doorway.

'Hey you,' he drawled.

'Sorry, who are you again?' I hissed, turning my back on him as I fiddled with the keys.

He came up behind me and enveloped me in a big hug. 'I know, I know,' he murmured in my ear as he held me tight so I couldn't wriggle away from him. 'I'm a self-obsessed jerk who's been neglecting his really cool girlfriend. I should be taken out back and horsewhipped.'

'You're going to have to do better than that,' I said grumpily although I was melting at the feel of Dylan's lean body pressed against me.

'Well I've got chocolate and some arty but romantic DVDs back home,' Dylan whispered. 'And best of all, I'm going to spend the next fourteen hours kissing you senseless.'

With some difficulty, I turned round so I could look at him. Dylan arched an eyebrow enquiringly. 'So am I forgiven?'

'I'll think about it,' I mock-sulked, which actually isn't that different from when I'm really sulking. 'I'm expecting some major crawling though. And present-buying. You might want to start pricing up tiaras.'

Dylan gave me a slightly evil smile, 'How about I make it up to you in kind.'

I thought about it for a moment. 'No, I'd rather have diamonds, I think. I'd get right on that if I were you.'

Dylan pushed me against the wall and placed his arms on either side of my head so I couldn't escape the wicked glint in his eyes as he took in my completely crap attempts to pretend that I wasn't about to make a pre-emptive bid on the whole senseless kissing arrangement.

'How about you use your lips for something other than pouting and I'm sure we can come to some arrangement,' he purred, before lowering his head.

I'm never going to persuade anyone to buy me a tiara.

9th December

Hey, sweet little diary. Did you miss me? There's a reason why I haven't written in ages, apart from the usual work/band/Dylan thing. I've been sorting out my big, exciting move! Not back to the folks because it's just not going to happen. I love them dearly but now I've had a taste of freedom it's too hard to go back to live with a woman who tries to button up my coat every time I leave the house.

I'm moving into my very own place! Kind of. I'm going to be living in the empty flat above the café with Poppy, Shona and Paul, because Shona and Paul are practically living together anyway and she feels the same way about the boys' bathroom as I do. Anna chucked out her last tenants 'cause they were non-rent paying slackers and is letting us have it cheap because we're so lovely and she doesn't want the building empty all night. Though she did make a muttered aside that it would be the only way that she could guarantee me and Poppy actually turn up for work on time. I can't imagine what she means.

Mum and Dad have been calmer about it than I expected. I have the sneaking suspicion that they actually like having the place to themselves. I think Dad must have told Mum that I'd be going to university in a few months anyway so if I did move back in it would only be delaying the inevitable and then she'd only get upset all over again when I moved out. And this way, they have Anna around to keep an eye on me, which is skewy logic on their part because she's only around when the café's open, leaving me to get up to a world of wrong after five o'clock most nights! Whatever. The good thing is they're paying my rent. It's a bit like a parentally-sponsored project to see how independent I really am.

D and I talked for two minutes about moving in together but came to the speedy conclusion that he'd kill me for leaving my clothes all over the floor, if I hadn't already killed him first for being too damn chirpy first thing in the morning.

I think we're well beyond that first part of going out together where we spent all our time hanging out and holding hands. Now, we both have our own stuff going on but it just makes seeing him even more exciting. If

I have to go a couple of days Dylanless, then when we do hook up it's like falling in love with him all over again. Seeing his face crack into this sunshine smile when he first catches sight of me, and realising that I'd forgotten just how green his eyes are or how I'd never seen him wear that T-shirt before makes me glad that he still has depths I've yet to explore.

God, I'm in danger of turning terminally sappy. I need to watch that.

17th December

So somehow I had to fit in working, band rehearsals and moving – hence even more lack of wordage in diary. I think Dylan's secretly relieved that we're not shacking up together although his toothbrush has permanent visitation rights, especially after we hauled my many goods and chattels into my little attic room and then had trouble getting the door shut. But it's going to be all kinds of good when he stays over and we don't have to worry that Poppy's mum or one of his flatmates is going to burst in on us doing something they'd rather not know we were doing. Even if it's only Dylan letting me paint his toenails.

'Do you think we're getting boring and coupley?' I asked him as he hung up my fairy lights and I unpacked my third binbag of clothes.

Dylan threw a balled-up pair of socks at me in protest. 'I make sculptures out of food and you have a theory about carrier bags being the next dominant species,' he pointed out with a smirk. 'I don't think boring is the right word.'

'Well not when you put it like that,' I said, after I'd had a moment to consider it. 'And we do our own stuff. I just worry that we're like as dull and middle-age-y as Prince William and Kate Middleton.'

'Nah! We're the anti-Wills and Kate,' Dylan shuddered. He turned to look at the rest of my things waiting to be unpacked. 'Explain to me again why you have so many dresses?'

19th December

We played our second gig last night at the Christmas party at my old college and got our first groupie – this fifteen-year-old kid from Cheadle Hulme who tried to snog Poppy after buying her a drink.

'Not while there's dogs on the pavement,' she snarled at him before flouncing off to find Jesse. That would be Jesse her new boyfriend, though he's very much on a thirty-day free trial even if he doesn't know it. (Our flat is just like the boys' old flat with Dylan, Paul and Jesse there all the time. It just smells less of boy and more of girl.)

Anyway, the gig: I think we're not so much about the songs and more about our stage outfits (we wore matching Barbie T-shirts and tutus over our jeans – well, it's a look) and the between songs banter. I think

Poppy wishes it was actually more about the songs but then she's going to have to get together with people who can actually play their instruments well instead of just about adequately.

After we came off stage, I dragged Grace over to Dylan to explain why it was necessary to have at least thirty vintage dresses when someone caught my eye.

'Grace!' I tugged at her arm. 'It's that boy! The one from outside the cinema.'

Dylan looked up. 'Oh that's Jack. He comes into Rhythm all the time.'

I nudged Dylan. 'Get him to come over!'

'Edie!' Grace said between clenched teeth. 'Stop it!'

Dylan winked at me and then waved at Jack.

'He's coming over,' I told Grace rather unnecessarily, but the pissy expression on her face was very amusing.

Jack shambled over. He's quite cute really. He has a thin face with these huge brown eyes and all this floppy blond hair, which he constantly pushes back. 'Er hi, Grace,' he said softly.

Grace grunted quietly.

'I'm Edie,' I shouted over the music, sticking out my hand so he could shake it. Good firm grip. 'So where do you know Grace from?'

'We're in the same English class,' Jack mumbled, peering at her from under his eyelashes, then looking away like he'd been caught shoplifting.

I smiled encouragingly. 'I'm having a housewarming cum Christmas party next week. You should come.'

Dylan shook his head and made the universal sign language for throat slitting at me but I ignored him.

Grace was staring stonily at the wall and Jack was gazing at Grace as if she was a big bar of chocolate suddenly come to life.

'So this party?' I prompted. Jack tore his eyes away from Grace.

'Er yeah, sounds cool,' he muttered.

'I'll give Grace an invite to give to you,' I promised before following Dylan into the crowd because he was clutching my hand so tightly that if I hadn't, he'd have had my arm off.

'Don't,' he said sternly, when we got to the bar and he decided that maybe it would be a good idea to stop cutting off my circulation.

'Don't what?' I asked innocently.

'Don't meddle.' He gave me one of his looks. This one is my least favourite because it manages to convey equal parts disapproval and disappointment. 'What do you want to drink?'

'Oh, don't be mad at me and anyway you were happy enough to call him over,' I fiddled with my fake tiara.

Dylan straightened it for me and ran his fingers through my hair. 'Just let Grace find her own boyfriend, OK?'

'But by then she'll be in her eighties and living on her own with loads of cats,' I protested.

Dylan threw up his hands. 'I give in. It's impossible to argue with someone who's wearing a tutu anyway. Undignified, you know?'

23rd December

Grace still hasn't forgiven me but I'm not going to let a little thing like that stop me.

'He's so sweet,' I told her the evening of my party, while she was helping me unpack carrier bag upon carrier bag of nibbles. The others had gone to the off-licence, though why it took five of them I don't know. I think it was a cunning plot to stick me with the vacuuming.

'I'm not listening!' she insisted.

I shook my head. 'Oh, please, you fancy him. He obviously fancies you. What's the problem?'

'It's, oh y'know, I've never, um even . . . kissed someone, I mean, a boy before,' Grace stuttered. 'Apart from Carter and he *so* doesn't count.'

'You don't have to snog him, talking would be good though.'

But Grace blushed for the millionth time and refused to say anything more.

And by the way, why did no-one tell me that it was Christmas in two days' time? I'm going to have to get all my presents from Sainsbury's and hope people think I'm being cute and ironic, rather than just a girl who left everything to the last minute.

23rd December (later)

Note to self: Being the hostess sucks. I barely had any time to get ready, in between dusting and cleaning and trying desperately to get into the bathroom while there was still hot water. If this is being independent, I'm not sure I like it very much.

I was still in the shower when the first people turned up and I had to do a lightning streak back to my room with my towel clutched in a death grip around me. I just had time to throw on jeans and Shona's new vintage satin blouse and a bit of make-up, instead of spending hours getting ready to look like I'd just thrown my look together. There is a *huge* difference.

I thought I'd mingle and pass around the odd plate of cocktail sausages and keep the party afloat with witty asides and tinkling laughter but actually I had to make sure everyone had a drink and didn't throw up on a non-easy-wipe surface. Plus I could see Grace and Jack on opposite sides of the living room not talking to anyone. I wanted to bash their heads together.

I was just making my millionth trip to the kitchen to see if any of the ice-cube bags in the freezer had actually iced up when I felt two hands reach round my waist and a warm mouth nip me lightly on the neck.

'Get off me!' I said crossly.

Dylan turned me round to face him. 'Oh it's you,' I muttered. 'This party is a disaster, Jack and Grace won't talk to each other and Will's been sick out of the window and I have no ice and . . .'

Dylan stopped my rant simply by backing me against the wall and kissing me till I couldn't think straight.

'What was . . . ?'

Dylan put a finger on my lips, took me by the hand and started leading me towards my room.

'But the party . . .' I protested as he opened the door.

Dylan gave me a wolfish smile. 'I thought you wanted to be not boring,' he purred.

Have I mentioned how much I love being independent?

31st December

It's been a weird, long year. This time last year, D was still with Veronique and there was that godawful party at the boys' flat where I managed to kiss Dylan *and* Carter within the space of fifteen minutes.

Then there were all those months of stress-inducing boy issues. Dylan and Carter played so many mind games with me, that it's quite miraculous that I still have some shreds of sanity left.

Even stranger is that I've forgiven Dylan. Really, really forgiven him, to the extent that I don't even bring it up when we argue. Sometimes I think that no matter how unpleasant it all got, it was necessary because it made me grow up. It made me stop being a wide-eyed kid with a crush on a boy and instead I'm becoming more like the girl I always wanted to be.

I'm a lot less whiny for starters. And I have plans that don't involve concocting ways to be in the same room as Dylan. I have big scary plans about life and what I want to be when I'm a grown-up, which I think is going to be pretty soon.

Like, I'm waiting to hear back from universities and have pretty much decided that I want to study English Literature and French and maybe even live in Paris for a year. And I love being in the band but I realise that it isn't going to be something that leads to fame, fortune and nubile, androgynous, young men throwing themselves at my designer-shoed feet. But my life is also about Dylan 'cause I honestly believe we're in it for the long haul. That it's not puppy love; or first love; or any of those other kinds of love that are never meant to last. I love him in so many different ways. In the way that he's a cute boy who's into me and kisses me until the world falls out from under my feet. And then I love him in this deeper way that kinda feels like he's a part of me, like we breathe to the same rhythm. So, I guess what I'm trying to make sense of here, albeit in a very rambly way, is that I never thought I'd get to the end of this year and there'd be someone, let alone Dylan, who'd mean more to me than I do.

15th January

Seems like I did a crap job of explaining why I love Dylan so much. He called me earlier and I think our phone conversation says what I can't. Like, that we're two people who totally get each other:

'Hello, Anna's Café, Edie speaking.'

'Hey you.'

'Hey you! I thought you were busy doing art boy stuff today.'

'I've got art boys' block.'

'What's art boys' block?'

'It's like writer's block but it only affects art boys. So are you busy or can you talk for a while?'

'God, this place is dead. Done the lunch crowd and Poppy's on washing-up and I'm re-filling the tomato ketchup tomato things.'

'You're what?'

'Y'know, those plastic red tomatoes that you put the ketchup in.'

'Oh, *those* tomato ketchup tomato things! So can you talk then?'

'Yeah, Anna's at the cash and carry and Italian Tony's popped off to the bookies.'

'I'm bored Edie. Can't you take the afternoon off and we could go and see a film or something?'

'Oooh! Yes! 'Cept, no, I can't just, like, leave.'

'You could say you were ill.'

'Yeah but Anna would come upstairs to see me. And there'd be no ill Edie and hell to pay.'

'I suppose that's the problem with living above the premises. Well, do you want to see *Moonrise Kingdom* after work? It's showing at the Rep. I'll pick you up.'

'Yeah, that'd be cool and then we could go for something to eat.'

'OK, soooo . . . c'mon talk to me.'

'Actually there was something I needed to talk to you about. But you're not going to like it.'

'That sounds ominous. You're not going to dump me, are you?'

'No! Don't be silly. It's just, well, I've got an acceptance letter from University College London for their French course.'

'Oh.'

'So say something.'

'I guess I knew this was going to happen but I just decided that if I didn't think about it, it would go away.'

'But it wouldn't start till the end of September and we're going to spend the summer in America and you've only got a year to go anyway and you said that you wanted to do a Masters degree in London so it would only be a year apart and I'd get really long holidays and we could still . . .'

'Jeez, Edie, you're going to start hyperventilating if you don't take a second.'

'Don't be mad at me, D.'

'I'm not mad at you, I just can't imagine what life would be like with you being more than fifteen minutes' walk away from me.'

'I know. I feel the same.'

'So what did your mum say about it?'

'She got all tearful about me moving to London and taking a job as a podium dancer in between lectures but I think she was also pleased.'

'At least I've got you till the end of September I s'pose.'

'You've got me after that as well.'

'Yeah, I know. Listen, I'm pleased for you but it'll take some time to get used to being Edieless.'

'Yeah, but I hear they've invented this wonderful thing called a train and if you give a nice man some money he'll let you go on his train all the way to London.'

'Hey, you're a real funny girl aren't you?'

' 'Sides September is ages away.'

'I know and I am going to have to kiss you and have wild, post-watershed sex with you even more now just to make up for all the times we can't spend together.'

'That's sweet.'

'I am sweet, that's why you're going out with me.'

'Oh yeah, that's why. I knew there had to be a reason. My God! I can't believe I didn't tell you this. Guess who came in here for lunch?'

'I don't know, Randolph the dog-faced boy?'

'Who? No! Grace and Jack!'

'On their own? Like, as a couple?'

'There was a whole bunch of them from college but they sat opposite each other.'

'Did they actually manage to speak whole sentences and maintain eye contact?'

'Not so you'd notice but it's early days. Don't start that whole matchmaking business again. You have to let them do their own thing.'

'Huh! If I let them do their own thing they'd be drawing their pensions before they'd even get round to saying "Hello".'

'Like us. If I hadn't been the one to make the first move we'd never have got together.'

'You're so not right. I had to pursue you relentlessly.'

'I was just playing hard to get. I'd have given in eventually.'

'Yeah, right . . . It's um, Dylan.'

'You still there, Edie?'

'Anna's back, have to go now.'

'Pick you up at five?'

' 'Kay. See you then.'

'See you. Oh and remember, lots of smooching on the menu tonight so remember your lip balm.'

'Bye D.'

'Bye Edie.'

Yeah, me and D, we're all right.

21st January

Dylan is driving me freakin' mad!

23rd January

Where am I? Back home *home* for the weekend where there is always ice cream in the freezer, no-one hogging the bathroom and a purry, purty cat currently sitting on my stomach so I can't actually see what I'm writing. Plus, there is no-one annoying the hell out of me.

29th January

I am not one of those girls who's only defined by her boyfriend. I have a life. A life that is going to send me into my own private room in a mental institution.

I have Poppy whinging at me about practising my guitar and her plans for domination of the upper reaches of the Top Twenty. I also have to witness the sight of Poppy and Jesse dry-humping in the kitchen when I'm trying to keep my cornflakes down.

I have work, work, work. And I'm sure all that grease is playing havoc with my pores. Plus, at least once every day some cheeky chappy thinks it hugely amusing to say, 'Cheer up, love, it might never happen' and because I want my tip I have to shoot him a big insincere smile that makes the sides of my face ache.

I have my parents banging on for England about tuition fees and halls of residence and how if I go to

America this summer I will definitely get involved in a drive-by shooting.

I have Grace avoiding me because she's too chicken to do something about the monster-sized crush that Jack has on her. Even if it's just to put him out of his misery.

And now I have Dylan moping and moaning at me from sun-up to sun-down (and actually for quite a long time after sun-down too if we're going to get technical about it) because in eight months I've got the audacity to want to leave town so I can get a degree.

OK, I've vented and I don't feel the least bit better.

11th February

I find getting up on Sunday mornings difficult. Some might say impossible. But Shona insisted me and Poppy and Grace got up at seven so we could go car-booting and buy quirky, exotic Valentine's Day presents for our boyfriends. She's just passed her driving test and wanted to feel the call of the open road beneath her mum's Honda Civic as we moseyed along the A roads to Blackpool.

We didn't talk in the car because Shona needed to concentrate and I was too busy having my whole life flash before me every time she braked suddenly. Then I'd get yelled at for flinching and therefore distracting her. It was a very tense journey. My legs were like half-set jelly by the time I got out of the car.

'So what are you going to get Dylan?' Shona asked me as we shuffled around the stalls set up in a school playground.

I shrugged. 'Something kitsch that will make him laugh,' I said. 'He's been in a complete funk ever since I told him I'd be going to study in London after the summer.'

'Yeah, he keeps gazing at her in a lovesick fashion and sighing heavily,' Grace added. 'It's really sweet.'

'I think I preferred it when she was mousy,' I hissed at Poppy who smirked.

'I'm going to look at clothes. I need a new stage outfit,' Poppy announced. 'C'mon Grace, heel.'

I got D the most wonderful present, plus we had these bacon butties from a transport caff on the way home that had to be one of the seven wonders of the modern world. Or does the modern world have eight wonders?

Crap! Now that's going to bug me for the rest of the day.

14th February (pre-brekkie)

Dylan stayed over and I woke him up by switching on his Valentine's Day present, a Fifties hula girl alarm clock. But even the plastic hula girl, hula-ing to *La Cucaracha*, failed to raise a smile.

'Unnnh,' he groaned, rolling over and burying his head in the pillow.

'Dylan!' I whined, nudging him.

'It's a cute present Edie, but every morning when I wake up, you'll be in London and it'll just remind me of you,' he sniffed before reaching under the bed, retrieving a small carrier bag and shoving it at me. He managed to do all this with his eyes still shut. And I'm the one who's not a morning person.

D had got one of his arty mates to make me a cute silver ring embossed with little pink enamel hearts. Plus there was a home-made card because Dylan always makes me cards to celebrate significant events and I'd throw the mother of all hissy fits if he decided to stop. This one had a cartoon of me on the front, wearing my tiara and he'd stuck bits of diamante on it. Inside he'd written, 'I love Edie like a fat kid loves cake.'

Aw, aw, and a thousand times aw.

I went to give him a big thank you kiss but he'd already gone back to sleep.

14th February (post-brekkie)

To tell you the truth, this Valentine's Day was always going to suck. It's the first Valentine's Day in three years when Dylan and I are actually *together* instead of either mooning over each other from afar/wishing that the other one didn't even exist/being non-committed kiss sluts (delete where applicable) which adds up to a lot of pressure *and* we're playing a gig tonight. Or more specifically, we're playing an anti-Valentine's ball.

When I dared to suggest that we turn the gig down so I could spend some relationship recuperation time with Dylan, the others spent the rest of the day mocking me harshly for being lame.

14th February (post-gig)

The first nine-tenths of our set was awful. Because it was an anti-Valentine's theme we had to play all our boys-are-evil-jerks songs, of which we have a fair few. As I tried to remember the chords for *He's A Loser* (*And He'll Never Be Any Good*) all I could see was Dylan sitting by the side of the stage looking like he was about to cry.

I couldn't bear it any longer.

When we finished the song, I stepped up to the mike. 'I know this is meant to be anti-Valentine's,' I said nervously, hoping that my knees knocking together wouldn't drown out the sound of my voice. 'And I'm down with that sentiment but I want to dedicate the next song to the sulky boy at the side of the stage. This one's for you, Dylan.' And it was completely unrehearsed but I started playing the thrash version of *This Girl's In Love With You* that me and Poppy had been mucking about with all week. Finally I got a smile out of him.

After the gig, we all piled into a club. Dylan had

cheered up. Like, to the power of one thousand. He pretended that he was embarrassed about having a song dedicated to him but judging by the way he kept pulling me into dark corners so he could give me these kisses which devastated my central nervous system, he was faking. I vaguely remember pulling Poppy and Grace onto the dancefloor so we could jump around to Azealia Banks when a huge bunch of flowers with legs walked up to Grace.

It was Jack hidden behind the biggest bouquet of mixed blooms I'd ever seen. If Dylan had done that, I'd have burst into soppy tears of happiness but Grace gave a horrified squeal and pushed the flowers back at Jack who promptly fled.

Then Poppy bawled out Grace loudly and publicly for being 'a selfish, emotionally crippled, thoughtless cow' and Grace fled. I should have been more concerned but Dylan was being sultry, which mostly involved nibbling my neck and telling me in no uncertain terms what he was planning to do to me when we got home, and Atsuko and Darby kept aiming their water pistols at us so I forgot all about Grace and Jack.

But (and it's a big but) when we got out of the club at some godforsaken hour, sitting on the wall opposite, sharing a bag of chips and looking morose were Grace and Jack. I think that's progress.

19th February

Dylan and I have just had what has to be the most scary, intense argument ever. 'Cept it never really got to be an argument; it whooshed out of control like someone had just thrown lighter fuel on a bonfire.

See, in between brooding and more brooding and, hmmm, brooding some more about my not-very-imminent move to London, Dylan found time to get hold of a copy of every US fly-drive brochure that's ever been written. I cashed in my Crimbo book tokens and bought a load of travel guides and we started to plan our amazing road trip adventure.

Actually we weren't getting very far. We knew where we wanted to go but planning out the route takes organisation, military precision and levels of concentration that neither of us seemed to possess.

'We should start in New York,' I said decisively, as I peered at the map I'd pinned to my corkboard.

'But New York's on the right and a lot of the places we want to go are on the left. Maybe we should start at the top in Seattle and work our way down.' Dylan traced his finger along the middle of the States.

I gave a frustrated groan. 'We have to do this in a scientific way? God! This is like being back at freakin' school.' I find in times of great stress that it helps to use not-quite-swear words.

'Maybe we should make a list of all the places that we want to go to and just draw a line that connects them together. And that's our route.' A very smug note was creeping into Dylan's voice, which I tried to ignore. It was not very becoming.

Instead I shrugged. 'Yeah, I guess that would work. Might be a pretty crooked line but, hey, I got nothing here.'

We started our US wishlist:

New York (both)
Seattle (both)
Portland (Dylan)
Las Vegas (both)
Palm Springs (Edie)
Hollywood (Edie)
San Francisco (Dylan)
Chicago (both)

That's as far as we got before we had a big argument because I had the audacity to point out that we'd have to go to other places to get to the places we wanted to go to. And then I might have had a teensy weensy little temper tantrum because it was getting really complicated and making my head hurt. I might even have thrown myself on the bed and pounded the pillows with my fists, while Dylan told me to grow up. But I didn't want to grow up so I lay there for a while, face down on the pillow and eventually Dylan stopped snarling at me, sat down on the edge of the bed and ignored me! He ignored me in my moment of pain. I sulked for about three more seconds and then, with great effort, managed to lift my head and say, 'Hey. What you doing?'

Dylan tilted his head and raised his eyebrows. 'I'm sorting through my wallet while I wait for you to stop regressing. You think you might be done soon?'

'Hunh,' I grunted and half sat, half rolled over so I could rest against Dylan's back, even though he's far too knobbly for comfort.

'Sorry, Eeds, I don't speak Neanderthal. Want to run that by me again?'

I reached up and kissed the back of his neck and tried to tug him round so we could have a cuddle but he was being all stiff and uncooperative.

'Give me a hug,' I ordered and then looked over his shoulder to see what was distracting him. 'What's that?'

Dylan was looking at a small, dog-eared photo. 'It's nothing,' he said far too quickly and tried to shove the picture back in his wallet but I was quicker and managed to get him in a weedy but effective headlock so I could snatch it away from him.

'Give it back!' Dylan twisted out of my hold but I scrambled off the bed and squinted at the photo. 'Is this you? Is that your mum and dad?'

Dylan pounced on me and held my arms by my sides so I couldn't move. 'I said, give it back!' he growled in my ear but he wasn't using his sex voice, he was using a very scary voice that made all the hairs on the back of my neck stand up and say hello.

He tugged the photo out of my hand, stuffed it in his jeans pocket and stomped towards the door, while I just stood there opening and shutting my mouth and wondering what the hell had just happened. I was still trying to process it, when I heard the front door slam. And even though I didn't have any shoes on, I suddenly had this gut feeling that something big and weird and potentially serious had happened so I ran down the stairs and out into the street in my bare feet because he couldn't leave just like that. And of course it had to be pelting down with rain. It just had to.

Dylan was a tiny but clearly bad-tempered little stick figure in the distance as I ran after him, the wet pavement stinging the soles of my feet. I was going to have to have a hardcore pedicure this weekend.

'Dylan! Hey! Hey!' I couldn't run and call out; I was no good at multitasking my oxygen supply so I concentrated on running as fast as I could.

Turns out I can run pretty fast. Who knew? It did help that Dylan had reached the bus-stop at the top of the road. He was peering at the timetable when I eventually caught up with him and practically collapsed onto the bench. I slumped there for a minute trying not to hyperventilate then Dylan folded his arms and regarded me stonily.

'I don't know what that was back there,' I panted, pushing wet rat's-tails of hair out of my eyes. 'If I crossed a line, I'm sorry.'

Dylan was doing a good impersonation of someone chewing on a wasp. He kept flaring his nostrils, which just made his cheekbones hollow out so his face looked like a death mask.

'I know that sometimes I don't quit when I should and I'm not even going to ask about the picture, but will you please just come back with me because I hate it when you get like this and we need to sort stuff out before it gets all grrrr and then we're not speaking and . . .'

'Give me one good reason why I should come back with you,' Dylan said flatly. Hadn't he heard a single word I'd been saying?

I threw him a pleading look, which totally underwhelmed him. But he did move nearer to me though it could have been because the rain was sheeting down like it does in pop videos and he wanted to get under cover. He shook out the collar of his leather jacket and looked down at the bottom of his jeans, which were soaked, just like mine. Plus my feet couldn't decide whether they were numb with cold or burning in pain.

Maybe a combination of the two.

I reached out a hand and placed it on Dylan's arm. 'Hey,' I said softly. 'This isn't the end of the world. We had an argument, don't make it into something that it isn't just 'cause you're angry about other things that you don't want to talk to me about.'

'And there she goes again.' Dylan's mouth twisted into a smile entirely lacking humour and I threw my hands up in defeat.

'Fine, whatever,' I bit out. 'Go on, disappear then if you're going to be like that.'

I got up and although all my muscles seemed to go into screaming spasms as I put my weight on what felt like the bleeding and battered soles of my poor feet, I was determined not to let it show.

Dylan was all stiff-backed like a furious cat as I inwardly shuddered at the painful walk back to the flat in the rain.

'See you then,' I said, like I didn't care, when I did care. I cared a whole lot and I didn't know if we were just having a fight and we'd make up so we could go to America and probably have more fights. Or if he'd just dumped me for something I didn't even know I'd done.

It was only 100 metres back up the road but it seemed like 500 miles. I also had a sudden sinking feeling akin to the *Titanic* hitting the iceberg when I realised I hadn't picked up my keys before I left and that I'd have to sit on the doorstep until one of the others got home.

It felt like someone was jabbing gazillions of red-hot

pokers, sharp knives and other pointy implements into the soles of my feet and I decided I was now far enough away from Dylan to exhibit huge signs of being in pain. I started crying, not that anyone would have been able to tell thanks to my fabulous impression of a drowned rat.

My front door was in sight but it seemed so far away . . .

'Jesus wept, Edie!' It sounded like Dylan or maybe I was suffering from a mild delirium but yes, it was Dylan scooping me up, which would have been very romantic in a completely embarrassing way if I wasn't cold, wet, in pain and with a ton of snot dribbling out of my nostrils.

'Put me down,' I bawled, even as I rested my head against his sodden chest. 'You'll give yourself a hernia.'

'You are a bloody pain in the arse, do you know that?' Dylan shouted at me. I nodded slowly because it did pretty much sum up the whole situation and his features shifted, melted, softened out and he kissed the top of my head before shifting me slightly.

'Can you get my keys out of my pocket?' said Dylan.

I managed to tug the button on his jacket pocket undone, though the wet leather was stubborn.

Dylan bent his knees so I could negotiate the lock.

'You can put me down now,' I told him once we'd got inside but Dylan ignored me and took a deep breath before he began to slowly climb the stairs. He shouldered the door to my room open, dropped me on the bed and walked out without saying a word.

I collapsed back on the pillow and then wished I hadn't as the tears that were still spilling from my eyes ran into my ears.

I thought Dylan had decided to carry on with the whole disappearing act but then I heard him opening drawers and cupboards in the kitchen.

When he came back I'd hauled myself into an upright position and was examining the very icky soles of my feet, which were filthy and bleeding.

'Don't touch them,' Dylan snapped, putting a bowl of water down on the floor. 'You'll just make it worse,' he added in a more mollifying way. 'I put some Dettol in here.'

I shuffled to the edge of the bed and gingerly put my feet in the almost scalding hot water. 'Ow, ow, ow!'

Dylan was scrabbling through the piles of junk on my dressing table until he found my tweezers, which he held aloft and my heart sank. 'Oh no!'

'You've got pieces of grit in there, which need taking out before they cause an infection,' he said sternly.

'I don't mind having an infection,' I informed him with a slight edge to my voice because I suddenly realised that this was All His Fault. 'I can live with an infection.'

'Yes,' said Dylan reasonably like he was talking to a retarded kid. 'Then you'll get gangrene and then they'll have to amputate your feet and you'll expect me to push you round in a wheelchair, so . . .' He clicked the tweezers together in a very uncomforting manner.

It hurt a lot. Really a lot. Dylan knelt in front of me with a towel on his lap and picked out all the tiny bits of glass and grit, while I bit my lip and clenched great handfuls of the duvet and tried not to scream. He kept making soothing noises and talking to me about . . . I can't really remember. I think it was where we were going to go when we got to the States, something about Memphis but I was too busy waiting for my endorphins to kick in to pay much attention.

Then he slathered my feet in Savlon, gave me a couple of Ibuprofen for the pain and tucked me into bed.

'Don't leave me,' I whimpered and my voice was all broken from crying. The words seemed to hang in the air between us, more loaded and desperate than three words had the right to be.

Dylan reached down and stroked my still damp hair back from my face. 'I'm not going anywhere. Well, just to the kitchen.'

I rubbed my cheek against the back of his hand. He felt cold. 'You promise?'

'I promise. And sorry for being such a drama queen,' he smiled ruefully.

I snuggled down under the covers. 'I thought *I* was the drama queen in this partnership.'

'We might have to take it in turns,' Dylan murmured, scratching his head. 'I'm a moody git, aren't I?'

'Yup, you really are,' I agreed.

He was back five minutes later with a cup of hot chocolate that he'd filched from Shona's secret stash that she thought no-one knew about. He'd even stolen some of her little marshmallows that were floating on the top.

'Yum,' I said happily as he placed the steaming mug on my bedside table and sat down next to me.

He had the photo in his hand.

'That's me when I was five,' he said, holding it out so I could see the blurred image of a pint-sized Dylan wearing naff clothes because it was the Nineties and people always wear naff clothes in those kinds of photos. 'That's my mum and that's my dad.' They were just smudged faces that told me nothing.

All of a sudden I wanted to know everything. Why his dad had walked out. When was the last time he saw him? What his mum looked like when she smiled. When did everything start going crazy? But I realised that I had to walk this path with baby steps and now wasn't the time. So I handed the photo back to Dylan. 'You looked cute,' I said and he gave me a grateful smile as I stroked my hand along the curve of his spine.

24th February

I managed to wear kitten heels today so I guess my feet are officially healed. Hurrah! Though I will miss a guilt-ridden Dylan waiting on me hand and foot.

Our living room became *the* hang-out while I was recovering. Which was slightly annoying when Poppy, Shona and I wanted to slump around in our PJs and watch *Friends* and talk about Jennifer Aniston's hair in a completely un-ironic, 'we're not actually as cool and edgy as we pretend to be' way.

Even Grace deigned to honour us with her presence. Truth be told, Grace has been pretty elusive ever since she bonded with Jack on Valentine's Night. I think she's fed up with me and Poppy badgering her for details on whether they've actually spoken/gone on a date/snogged.

'God, you two are like something from the Salem witch trials!' Dylan snorted, having witnessed the pair of us in action.

'We're just looking out for her,' Poppy protested, looking completely unrepentant. 'Did I tell you I've asked Jack to roadie for us?'

'But Dylan and Jesse are doing it,' I said. 'We're not paying him.'

Dylan shifted on the sofa. 'Well, you're not paying us either, remember?'

Poppy looked indignant. 'Why should we? Jack's doing it because I told him that Grace was coming.

We should get more lovesick roadies, they're very cheap.'

Dylan stood up. 'I've got to go. I'll see you on Saturday when I roadie for you out of the goodness of my heart,' he said morosely.

I jumped up in a manner that wouldn't hurt my feet so we could have a cheeky little kiss but Dylan muttered something about having to dash and dashed.

'What the hell is the matter with him?' Poppy asked.

I sank back down on the sofa. 'Huh! It's London, isn't it? He's all depressed about it again.'

'But we're only going to play a gig!'

'Yeah but in a few months I'll be moving there permanently,' I scowled. 'No wonder I've got a rash!'

I forgot to mention the rash. I'm covered in patches of itchy red spots. It's not even anything dramatic like chicken pox or an allergy to second-hand, man-made fibres. Mum took one look at it when she came round and made me pull up my jumper because my flesh is like her own personal property and diagnosed stress rash.

'Not that you have anything to be stressed about,' she declared in a very annoying manner. 'You don't know the meaning of being stressed.'

Which, hello! I mean, you try working the lunchtime rush when the deep fat fryer's on the blink. Or waiting outside a cinema for a sculpture-obsessed Dylan who's completely forgotten the time. Or there's the gig in London with your band in a week's time and you feel like throwing up every time you think about it.

So like I said I have a rash.

3rd March

We travelled down to London in the café van. Dylan was driving but let Jesse ride shotgun while the rest of us sat in the back and became moderately hysterical.

'But what if no-one turns up or during one of the quiet songs someone heckles us?' fretted Atsuko.

'Or the venue's been double booked?' added Darby.

'Or we suddenly forget all the chords and all the words to all our songs?' I chipped in, rubbing my rash-ridden chest.

'Firstly, stop scratching, Edie,' Poppy said angrily. 'And secondly, we are going to rock. We don't need the approval of snotty London people and we look . . .'

'Dylan!' Atsuko moaned. 'Turn up the radio, we can still hear Poppy.'

Of course that sent Poppy into a mammoth sulk, Dylan was already sulking, Grace and Jack were, well being Grace and Jack, me, Atsuko and Poppy were manic and Jesse was oblivious to it all.

Weirdly, the gig didn't suck too much. But what happened afterwards did.

We decided to stay to see the other bands even though Dylan was muttering under his breath and clenching his jaw a lot. Clench, unclench. Clench, unclench. It was like a metronome stuck in his cheek. I decided to let him get on with it and wandered off to chat to the guitarist in the other support band who'd been wanting to have a tedious muso conversation about effects pedals. Boys, eh? All of a sudden I felt a hand wedge itself under my armpit and pull me away.

'Dylan!' I hissed. 'Get off!' I tried digging my heels in but Dylan had obviously got in touch with his inner caveman and was having none of it.

'We're going, I'm bored and I'm not staying here to watch people hit on my girlfriend,' Dylan snarled, dragging me vanwards while the others straggled along behind.

Dylan ignored me all the way back to Manchester but ended up having to stay over because he'd left his keys at home. We lay in bed, not talking or touching and I couldn't help but wonder if Dylan was bored and this whole London thing was just an excuse to dump me.

I scratched my arm and turned over.

'Edie, you awake?' Dylan said, rolling over and switching on the lamp.

I shielded my eyes. 'Well I am now.'

'Look, I'm sorry. I'm bad and I'm moody and you don't deserve it,' he murmured.

I felt icy fingers of fear trace a path down my back.

'Are you about to split up with me?' I hiccuped.

Dylan sat up and looked at me incredulously. 'Of course not! Come here.'

He pulled me towards him and wrapped me up in his arms. 'It's just I know I should be making the most of the next few months but it's hard. I feel like you're slipping away from me.'

'I'm so not!' I insisted. 'I'm still here and even when I'm not, I will be. Hang on, that didn't come out right.'

I felt Dylan chuckle. 'I know what you mean.'

'It's just we seem to be having arguments all the time lately.' I sat up and heard Dylan mutter as one of my elbows accidentally jabbed him. 'Are you getting bored with me?'

Dylan shifted so he was curled around me, his head on my tummy. 'You're never boring,' he said feelingly. 'Never. I just wish sometimes that we could stay the same forever. Like I could pause us so we're just stuck in the moment because when I look ahead there's all this change.'

'I know. But if we love each other, we should be able to make it, you know? You do still love me, right?'

'God, you know I do. Never loved anyone like I love you. You're my sunshine girl,' he whispered fiercely and I felt something tight suddenly give way in my chest. Like, I'd been holding my breath for too long and all of a sudden I could exhale. Sometimes Dylan knows exactly the right thing to say.

'Yeah, well I love you too,' I mumbled far more

prosaically. 'Though you've been behaving like a bit of a jerk lately.'

I twisted away from him so I could get at a particularly itchy spot on my ankle.

'Will you stop scratching that flaming rash if I promise to stop being such an idiot?' Dylan asked me.

'I don't know,' I mock pouted. 'It really itches.'

'Maybe I could help you with that?' Dylan said with a mock leer and when I squealed and made like I was going to get as far away from him as humanly possible, he pounced on me.

15th March

I think the coolest thing is just about to happen. Just going to meet D and some art boy mates of his who are on this exchange from the US and we shall see!

18th March

Yay! Instead of forking out vast sums of money to hire a car and then fork out even more vast sums of money for every mile that we do in it, we're getting a car for nothing! Nought pence! Nada! Nix!

It's a little bit complicated but one of the American art boys, Lewis, has this little sister who's going to university in New Mexico this autumn and they need someone to drive his other brother's car from New York to LA where the family lives. And it looks like it's going to be us.

D has to fax over his driving licence and passport to their dad but it seems like they were going to pay this company to drive the car anyway. It doesn't hurt that they've been letting Lewis kip on the lads' sofa for a week after his girlfriend kicked him out. And it simples things up so much. Like, now we know that we have to start in New York and finish in LA. It's only the bit in the middle that's the problem.

Plus, we're saving a stack of cash.

23rd March

D and I had Sunday lunch with my oldsters today. It's getting to be a regular occurrence. I think Mum has a bit of a crush on D, which is actually too ewww to dwell on. She lets him call her Alice and everything.

We took round our guidebooks and the draft of the itinerary for Dad to have a look at, which so was not a good idea.

When I told him that we were borrowing a car, he sniffed and said, 'Oh dear.'

And when I tried to explain that I'd planned out our route ten times, he brought up the thorny topic of the D grade I got for my Geography GCSE and then repeated, 'Oh, once again, dear.' Being a considerate kind of girl, I left him and Dylan to it. Mum and I curled up on the sofa and watched *West Side Story* because men they do the boring map stuff and women they watch the musicals and sniffle in the sad parts.

Eventually Dad and Dylan appeared with a new draft of the itinerary, which apparently is far more logical and time-sensitive than the one we had done. Whatever!

Mum muttered something about maybe getting me a credit card for emergencies but I think she regretted it when I sat bolt upright and squealed!

'Can it be a gold card? Or, oooh, a platinum card? Will it have my name on it? What's going to be my credit limit?'

'I said maybe,' and the colour had drained out of her face as I subsided back on to the cushions.

'Was it the squealing that made you change your mind?' I asked but she just patted my hand.

3rd April

Dylan and I were looking for a new thrill and now we've found it. Bingo! Cheap drinks, chunky felt-tips and the opportunity to win cash prizes. Plus we are the hottest, youngest and prettiest people in the place by about fifty years. What more could a girl want?

We haven't told anyone else, it's our guilty secret that once a week we like to spend serious down time among grannies wearing velour leisure suits.

So there we are sidling out of the Mecca, planning to blow our winnings on a Chinese when who do we see but Grace and Jack coming towards us.

'What are you doing here?' Grace and I both asked each other guiltily.

'Oh Edie needed the loo so we popped in to the bingo hall,' said Dylan blithely. He's a shameless liar. It's one of the things I do so love about him.

'So what *are* you two doing together?' I asked again. 'In this lonely, none-of-us-ever-come-here part of town.'

'We bumped into each other . . .'

'Somebody at college is having a party.'

I smirked. 'Do you want a minute to get your stories straight?'

But Dylan took pity and dragged me off when it became obvious that Grace and Jack weren't going to spill.

'Stop tormenting them,' he admonished me as we tucked into our crispy aromatic duck and egg fried rice.

I pulled a face. 'I'm not. I just want them to admit that they like each other and, I don't know, engage in a mild PDA.'

Dylan rolled his eyes and muttered under his breath about meddling and how no good could come of it.

10th April

I think Grace and Jack are stalking me. I was in the music shop picking up some new strings when I bumped into Jack eyeing up guitars he couldn't possibly afford. He looked at me nervously and tried to hide behind a speaker stack.

'It's OK, Dylan's told me off,' I said. 'I'm not even going to mention *her* name.'

At the non-mention of Grace's name, Jack went all glassy eyed and asked me if I wanted to go for a coffee.

It took him two hours and five cappuccinos to finally spit out that he fancied Grace but wasn't sure how she felt about him and I'd worked that out thirty seconds in. He looked at me expectantly.

'Be bold,' I cried boldly. 'Stop pussyfooting about and let her know. Dylan and I wasted two years faffing about.'

Yes, it's very easy to be a relationship guru when you've been through what I have.

Then later on Dylan and I were taking advantage of a Poppy and Shona-free flat to get horizontal on the sofa when the doorbell rang. We carried on kissing furiously and grabbing at each other's clothes but someone was leaning on the flaming bell. It was Grace.

'I'm so confused,' she managed to bite out before plonking herself down between the pair of us.

Dylan and I had to make concerned faces while Grace whinged on for several millennia about how miserable Jack was making her because he didn't seem to be interested. I was close to jumping out of the window to get away from her when I heard Dylan inviting Grace to dinner.

'I can't take a repeat performance,' I moaned once we finally got rid of her.

Dylan arched an eyebrow. 'Oh Edie you have no faith in me,' he said in a mock-hurt way. 'We invite Jack too, fill their faces with food, dim the lights and stand well back. It won't fail.'

And he says that I interfere?

17th April

Dylan's cunning plan also involved sticking me with the cooking, so I decided to kick it old skool.

The fish fingers and mashed potato surprise might not have been up to Jamie Oliver's standards but made everyone laugh. True, Grace and Jack didn't actually talk to each other but they seemed pretty chilled. I couldn't work out how they managed to make arrangements to hang out with each other outside bingo halls if they never actually spoke to each other or made eye contact. It was very strange. Dylan obviously thought it was too as he was staring at them like they were a particularly mesmerising art installation. Until I kicked him. Plan B couldn't come a moment too soon.

'Time for Twister!' I insisted firmly once everyone had finished the strawberry Angel Delight.

Dylan groaned and I shot him a look that suggested

there would be no smoochies if he didn't look enthusiastic.

'Great! Twister! My joy is now complete,' he drawled with an entirely uninfectious lack of enthusiasm. 'I think me and Edie will go first.'

Grace and Jack bonded bigtime as they manned the controls and told Dylan off for cheating and tickling me. They were all shouty and giggly and so cute together that if I hadn't been full of fish fingers and Angel Delight I'd have eaten them all up.

I expected great things from their turn on the Twister mat but the minute they had to contort round each other, things got all stifled again. Grace was bending backwards with her leg stuck out and Jack was leaning over her when Dylan spun the wheel and ordered Jack to move his left leg to blue. But as he was trying to move it, he wobbled and he shook and finally he collapsed . . . on top of Grace.

It was so not of the good. They lay there for a second, tried to catch their breaths and then Grace's fists drummed furiously on Jack's back.

'Get off me,' she shrieked. Jack scrambled to his feet and was out of the front door before I had time to blink. And Grace raced to the bathroom and locked herself in.

Oh dear.

I'm giving up on this match-making thing. It's really

not worth the aggravation or slaving away over a hot stove for twenty minutes.

25th April

Dylan's been asked to exhibit at this young artists' exhibition thingy. It's a mucho big deal. Apparently, he's the first undergraduate to ever be asked to exhibit. I am so proud of him.

He's decided that he wants to do all these photos of me and Poppy for the exhibition. I thought this would mean that Poppy and I could plaster ourselves in make-up and wear our most frou-frou frocks but Dylan keeps shoving his lens in our just-woken-up faces and encouraging us to do suicidal things like cycle towards him down steep hills on windy days.

Well, it makes him happy, the little freak.

7th May

Dylan came to our band rehearsal and instead of lugging amps around and generally making himself useful he made me forget chords as he spent half an hour trying to shoot my hand and the 'I am a princess' sticker on my guitar.

'Can you move your hand faster?' he shouted at me while I tried to master the rather difficult bridge (muso term for the linky bit between the chorus and the verse) in *Living In The 0161*.

'Stop it,' I hissed.

'Oh, do that again,' Dylan mumbled, adjusting his focus. 'It looks good when you glare.'

'Poppy!'

'Don't distract her, arsewipe. I know it's pretty easy to do but don't.'

Poppy draped her arm around my shoulders and gave Dylan one of her patented death stares while I smirked at him. Dylan was undeterred and clicked away. 'Oh, that's great. It's very, y'know, girl gang.'

Then Poppy went really red and then really pale before taking Dylan's neck in her patented Vulcan grip (all I know is it hurts) and frogmarched him off the premises while I heard Darby say to Atsuko, 'Dylan's turning into a total art geek.'

20th May

Dylan's practically living in his dark room and surfacing only for microwaveable snacks. It's nice to have some me time. I tumbled out of bed very, very late, pulled on jeans and a halterneck (yay for almost summer) and mooched off to the cinema to see a Tom Hardy double bill at the Rep with Poppy. It was nice to have a bucket of popcorn to myself (Poppy doesn't like getting the little bits caught between her teeth) but I missed Dylan not holding my hand or stretching out his long legs and getting told off by the person sitting in front of him.

When we emerged blinking into the sunshine,

Poppy made her excuses and left. 'Jesse lost a bet last night, he has to be my slave for the next twenty-four hours,' she informed me, completely deadpan.

'Can you make him clean the kitchen floor and, oooh, get my hairslide out from the back of the fridge?' I demanded, digging through my bag so I could switch my moby back on.

I looked up to see an absolutely porno smile on Poppy's face. It should have had an 18 certificate. 'I've got plans for him that don't involve the fridge. Though maybe the contents of the fridge.'

'Urgh! Over-sharing! Please say you're going round to his because I do not want to see anything that might give me nightmares.'

But Poppy just laughed, gave me a kiss on the cheek and sauntered off. Meanwhile, I had five text messages from Grace telling me to call her.

'What's up?'

'Oh, everything,' she sighed. 'Can I come round? If Poppy's not going to be there . . .'

'She's over at Jesse's. OK, come over and could you stop at KFC on the way?'

21st May (the wee small hours)

Grace has crashed out on Poppy's bed, worn out by self-inflicted emotional torment. Turns out that she's being all weird about the whole Jack thing 'cause she's never had a boyfriend and was traumatised by the kiss forced on her by Carter, my evil ex.

'Jack's not going to wait forever,' she sobbed. 'But I'm so scared.'

'But Jack's really gentle,' I protested. 'He'd never make you do stuff you didn't want to do.'

'Yeah, but I'm so useless at talking to people, I'm so boring. I wish I was like you and Poppy,' Grace sniffled. I hope she wasn't getting snot on Poppy's pillow because then she'd really have something to cry about.

I nudged her leg with my foot. 'You're not boring! But you have to stop comparing yourself to other people. When I first moved here I was so shy. Every time Dylan looked at me I'd get this full-on, all over body blush.'

Grace gave me a trembly smile. 'Really? 'Cause now, you pretty much boss him about.'

'Yeah and I do not. But when I lived in Brighton I used to go to this disco on Saturday nights and always ended up kissing this science nerd with a pocket protector because he was the only guy who didn't call me "Weedy Edie".'

'So what you're saying is . . .'

'What I'm saying is that you won't feel like this forever, Gracie. 'Cause Jack can see the inner you and that's why he likes you.'

And then we both sighed in a moment of true girly bonding. It was very beautiful.

26th May

Dylan has disappeared. Someone who sounds a bit like him can sometimes be persuaded to come to the phone to jaw on about developing and hanging photos. Note to self: art boys, freaky. Being an art widow, I had a big Saturday night out with my girls, which ended up with us playing footie on a dual carriageway at two in the morning.

29th May

Weird! Just seen Grace for the first time since our big talk and she seems to have reached some kind of Zen-like state of inner tranquillity.

'How's the whole Jack thing?' I asked her, expecting yet another tearful tirade but she smiled serenely and told me that she had it under control.

Under control? Well, I guess I don't have to worry any more.

5th June

I've had to sort out all the roadtrip stuff because Dylan is emotionally and geographically unavailable. Luckily Shona helped 'cause she's very practical. Also Dad phoned Lewis's dad to talk Dad to Dad and all systems are go!

I took Dylan round some food and stayed long enough to hand it to him, before he pushed me out of the front door.

'I still love you,' he muttered through a mouthful of cheese sandwich. 'But this is going to be a surprise so get the hell out of here.'

And they say romance is dead.

11th June

Grace is weirding me out. Now that she's not banging on about Jack at every conceivable moment, it's impossible to get hold of her. Every time Poppy or me ring her she's on the interpipe and you get grunts instead of intelligent conversation. Take today fr'instance.

Me: 'So Grace have you still got my baby-blue skinny jeans?'

Grace: 'Um, yeah.'

Me: 'You seem a bit distracted.'

Grace: 'No.'

Me: 'You're on the internet, aren't you? Again.'

Grace: 'What? No, I'm listening to you.'

Me: 'I can hear you typing. What are you doing? You're either on G Chat or looking at pictures of Justin Bieber, you saddo.'

Grace: 'I'm not. I'm listening to you. What was that about Justin Bieber?'

Aaaaargh! That's me screaming via the medium of the written word.

15th June

Dylan's just as bad. He's emerged at last but spends all

his time at the gallery where the exhibition is taking place. And won't even give me the address. I might just as well not exist.

23rd June

Forget what I said about Grace and Dylan. All that seems to pale into insignificance after what Poppy has just done. She suddenly announced at rehearsal tonight that she's organised a tour for us. Which would be great if a) she'd bothered to let us know and b) the tour wasn't in August which is when I'll be road-tripping across the US of A with Dylan.

'But this is more important,' Poppy had screamed when I pointed that out.

'You knew about America,' I insisted. 'And did you think I was going to give up on my future and getting a degree to stay here and do this?'

'You're just one of those sappy girls who are more interested in their boyfriend than being loyal to your friends,' Poppy had screamed even louder. 'And how was I to know you were actually serious about your stupid road trip? I thought it was another of your ridiculous plans that never goes anywhere.'

'Yeah, well at least I don't waste all my time on stupid fantasies that I might be famous,' I'd yelled back. 'It's been fun Poppy, but let's face it, we're crap! We can't play more than three chords between us.'

Poppy had looked to Atsuko and Darby for some

support but they'd wisely decided to be someplace that was else.

'Fine, fine then,' she'd spat. 'We'll do this tour without you and to save you the trouble of formally quitting the band, I'll do it for you. You're out. You can't play the guitar for crap anyway.'

I'd tried to think of something really wounding and sarcastic to say but I couldn't think of anything. It hadn't mattered though 'cause Poppy was already stomping towards the door.

23rd June (later)

'You'll make it up,' Dylan assured me as I lay whimpering on his bed. 'You two are always having rows.'

'This wasn't a row,' I argued. 'It had scenes and acts and walk-on parts.'

'Well, she shouldn't take it on herself to sort out a month-long tour and think it would be a really nice surprise.'

'You're not just saying that 'cause I'm your girlfriend and you have to take my side?' I mumbled.

Dylan stopped looking for his favourite 2B pencil and climbed on to the bed so he could spoon in behind me.

'Edie, I've called you out plenty of times when you've been hissy-fitting about nothing,' he said, kissing the back of my neck. 'But Poppy . . . she's just all "nothing must stop me in my plan for world domination". If I can accept that you have to do things even if they don't fit in with what I want, then so can she.'

'I hate her,' I said, because I'd suddenly turned into a ten-year-old.

'No you don't.'

'No, I don't but she's really pissed me off,' I conceded. 'And I'm not talking to her until she says she's sorry.'

Dylan can be very wise occasionally so he didn't say anything at all. He didn't even make a snorting noise, he just carried on kissing the back of my neck.

27th June

I'm beginning to think that Mrs Poppy must have taken lots of mind-altering drugs when she was pregnant with her two daughters. Because they are both complete mentalists.

Like, Poppy won't even speak to me, let alone be in the same room as me. If I'm not at Dylan's or she's not at Jesse's, she'll walk out rather than be in the kitchen when I'm making a cup of tea. I'm not going to apologise for the sake of making it up and a peaceful life because none of this is my fault.

For once.

And as for Grace! Turns out that her and Jack are Skype dating because they don't feel they're ready for the real thing.

If you put Grace and Poppy together, you might possibly have one almost sane girl.

1st July

Poor, poor Dylan. He spends weeks taking photos of me and Poppy for his first big art exhibition. He spends even longer thinking up a name for it: *Edie and Poppy: The only colour in this world is love* (um, whatever). And when he unveils his big surprise, one of the girls is absent and the other one (that'd be me) tries to smile and then goes to the Ladies so she can get a grip on herself before she starts bawling her eyes out.

Eventually I emerged. Dylan was talking to one of the exhibition organisers so I wandered around and looked at the photos. As far as I could tell they were a love story. A love story about me and Poppy and how cool it is to be a girl. Dylan had captured us doing all the things we loved to do together: playing our guitars and putting on make-up and sharing clothes and eating ice cream and just generally hanging out and being girl-shaped. Plus we looked smudgily beautiful.

I have to sort out this Poppy thing.

6th July

Poppy's put 'guitarist wanted' ads up all over town that say 'Must be able to play more than three chords.' She's like an evil genius when it comes to hurt.

7th July

Dylan and I spent last night doing the final draft of our road trip, it took hours. We're going to start in New York and drive to LA via Chicago and Seattle and San Francisco. That's Dylan's deal, the driving whereas I'm Miss Map Reader.

'That's the most money I've ever spent on anything,' I said to Dylan in a shaky voice, as we came out of the travel agent's having forked out a cool £1000 on plane tickets and about every form of insurance it's possible to buy.

Dylan grinned and took the tickets from me. 'Not that I don't trust you but I'll look after these.'

'We're going to America!' I squeaked, hugging Dylan. 'We're actually going to do it.'

Dylan gently brushed his lips against mine. 'I can't believe we had a plan and saw it through. We must be getting mature.'

9th July

Grace came over to see me today to help me move my stuff back home. Shona and Paul have agreed to drive it down to London in time for me to start at university. I swear, my entire life is about organising complex and detailed stuff. Any more of it and the entire back of my head will cave in.

I was trying to shove things in bags and boxes and wasn't planning on listening that attentively to Grace banging on about Jack for, like, hours but she was *very* twittery and twitchy. I thought it was Jack-related but when I finally asked her what was up after I'd boxed up the last of my books, she flopped down on the bed and announced that she wanted to try out for the guitarist job in Mellowstar.

'I know all the songs and I can play a guitar but Poppy won't even let me audition,' she protested. 'She's such a bitch at the moment.'

'Well I'd offer to talk to her but I don't think it would help,' I said. 'I could talk to Atsuko and Darby though?'

Grace sat up eagerly. 'Now?'

I sighed and reached for the phone. 'OK, I guess now would do.'

Atsuko and Darby were surprisingly up for the idea of Grace in the band. Something to do with Poppy asking this girl whose boyfriend they'd both snogged if she wanted to join. I really didn't want to go into the details. They both promised they'd out-vote Poppy, as long as Grace knew the songs.

The packing went out of the window as I spent the afternoon drilling Grace in the finer art of playing the same three chords that we used in all our songs. But, like, in different combinations.

'I think you've got it,' I said after five hours. 'Well, you're better than I ever was, not that that's saying much.'

Grace squeezed my hand. 'Oh, Edie, I'm really going to miss you. You're like the sister I wanted, instead of the evil bitch queen sister I got.'

'Poppy's OK,' I muttered. 'She's just a bit more driven than the rest of us. Makes her mouth say nasty things before her brain gets in on the act.'

Grace nodded. 'I s'pose. Well, all I need now is a guitar.'

I looked at the guitar that I'd spent months saving up for and Dylan had painted pink for me. I picked it up, feeling the weight of it in my hands.

'I want you to have it,' I said to Grace who stared at me with her mouth wide open. 'It's not like I'm going to need it. I'm going to be busy with the book learning.'

'But are you, I mean . . .'

'Look, take it and get out of here,' I mumbled, feeling tears prick the back of my eyes. 'I have packing that is so not done.'

15th July

My last day at the café. Never again will I have to be splashed by the evil deep fat fryer. Or be told to 'crack a smile' by the gang of builders that come in for their special breakfasts every morning. Italian Tony won't be able to tug on my pigtails and Anna won't take breakages out of my paypacket any more.

So why do I feel so sad? Probably because, even

though she's spent the last few weeks glaring at me from behind the coffee machine, I won't get to spend all day with Poppy.

'Are you ever going to speak to me again?' I asked her today when she'd come into the storeroom to get some mayonnaise. I was skulking in there because I knew the others were writing in my 'surprise' Bon Voyage card.

'I don't talk to people who dump on their friends,' she growled. Then she stuck her chin out, which means there's no reasoning with her and I had to let it go.

She didn't even sign my card.

I moved back to the 'rents today too. I know I should be looking forward to Edie And Dylan's Road-Tripping USA Adventure™ but it's also important that I feel sad about this part of my life ending. There's all these little things that have made up part of my day for the last year and now they're not going to happen ever again. The future's out there, it's like just within my reach but it's also scary. It's this big leap into the unknown and I'm not sure how far I can jump.

15th July (later)

We had a very low-key leaving do in the pub this evening, probably because there were parents there. Even Jesse was quite subdued with Mrs Poppy around.

Dylan and I sat there holding hands and not really saying much apart from the odd, 'Do we need to get travel sickness pills?' and 'Don't forget to phone up and sort out the International Roaming on your mobile.' Plus, my mum watched every sip I took so I couldn't even get hammered, which is what I really felt like doing.

It was actually the most boring leaving do in the history of leaving dos until Poppy suddenly stormed in, followed by an unhappy-looking Grace.

I cowered against Dylan. 'Oh no, this isn't going to be good,' I muttered as Poppy looked around wildly, clocked me and marched over.

'How dare you go behind my back!' she screeched. 'It's my band and I decide who's in it.'

I could *hear* Dylan rolling his eyes, I swear. He gave my leg a reassuring squeeze under the table but then became very interested in the contents of his pint glass.

Grace was standing behind Poppy and mouthing the word 'sorry' at me as Poppy carried on carrying on.

'I was going to get Grace to join all along,' she ranted – or lied, to be more accurate. 'I'm so glad you won't be around to stick your nose where it's not wanted.'

'Poppy, don't be like this,' I said quietly, in the vain hope it might calm her down. 'I don't want to fight with you any more.'

'Yeah, well you're just a lightweight,' she sneered. 'I don't need you, you hold me back.'

And when I was lying in bed and trying to sleep because I was going on holiday in a few short hours, all I could think about was the venom in Poppy's voice.

Road Trip!

16th July

It rained practically all the way to London, almost as if the raindrops were little messengers from some higher being telling us to get the hell out of England.

Dylan had managed to get all our stuff into the back of the Mini after forbidding me to take more than one suitcase and then standing over me as I re-packed and re-packed.

'Who died and made you boss of all the luggage?' I'd bitched at him after he'd pointed out that I didn't need more than two pairs of sunglasses and I certainly wasn't going to wear a winter coat. Even my mother had been impressed at the way Dylan had managed to halt my 'I don't do travelling light' speech after only two minutes, before she went back to sniffing loudly and making more sandwiches.

'You're leaving on a jet plane. Don't know when you'll be

back again,' Paul warbled from the back seat. I craned my neck so I could look round at him and Shona who'd volunteered to drive Dylan's car back to Manchester and Grace who was wedged between them and had come along for the ride.

'I can't believe I had to get up at five,' moaned Shona for the tenth time.

I nodded sympathetically. 'I hear you.' I looked at my travel notebook for confirmation and then added: 'But we have to check in at 14.00 hours GMT and the plane leaves at 16.40 hours GMT and we should get in to New York at 19.00 hours, EST – that stands for Eastern Standard Time.'

'You want to run that by us one more time?' Dylan chuckled.

'I'm sorry, I just don't want us to be late,' I said. 'Does anyone want a sandwich? The Mothership was up at four this morning making them. She even cut the crusts off.'

Paul leaned forward. 'Well, pity to let them go to waste.'

Silence.

'Can we stop for a pee break at the next services?'

'No! We won't make it. It's already eleven o'clock now and we've got miles to go.'

'Dylan! Edie's gonna make me wet myself.'

'Edie, don't make Shona wet herself.'

'It's not my fault! I hope our road trip car goes faster than your Mini.'

'Hey, Dylan, Edie, you do know there's a fifty-five miles per hour speed limit in America?'

'Yeah, right!'

'No, really.'

'Are you sure?'

'Yeah, it says so right here in your guidebook.'

'Oh. Hell!'

More silence.

'So how much money are you taking with?'

'God, Paul, it's so rude to ask about money. You don't have to answer that.'

''Kay.'

'So give us a ball-park figure.'

'I saved up about £3000 from tips and wages and guilt-tripping various relatives.'

'Dylan?'

'I have money from when my dad left. Don't even think about asking any more questions.'

'Oh, and my 'rents gave me a credit card for emergencies.'

'And a dictionary definition of what an emergency is.'

'Shut up Dylan, no they didn't. An emergency could be anything from the car breaking down to, um, my roots coming through.'

'Your parents are so deluded about you, Edie. I'm one of your best friends, right?'

'Right! Aw, thanks Shona.'

'Yeah, but I'd still never give you a credit card.'

London

16th July (later)

Eventually, after one pee break and a tense moment when it seemed as if the engine had over-heated, we got to Heathrow. With an hour to spare.

'I could yell at you about the extra hour I could have had in bed but you're leaving and I feel sad so I won't,' said Shona as Paul and Dylan got our suitcases out of the boot.

'We could get a coffee before you go?' I suggested. 'Dylan?'

Dylan nodded. 'Let's check in and dump our cases, then get coffee and food. Lewis says they don't do bacon butties in America.'

'Who's Lewis?' Shona wanted to know as we walked into the terminal.

'This American guy who's on Dylan's course, whose brother we're staying with in New York and taking the car from,' I said vaguely. 'I think that's right . . . What?'

Shona was giving me one of her patented 'engage your brain cell right now' looks.

'Do you think that you should have organised a proper fly-drive holiday?' she asked bluntly. 'This all sounds a bit, y'know, doomed to failure.'

'Don't listen to Edie,' Dylan said rather unsupportively. 'It's all cool. Frosty cool. Parentally approved. We're driving the car to LA so their little sister can take it with her when she goes to university.'

'In New Mexico,' I added helpfully.

'Oh well that makes everything so much clearer,' Shona muttered sarcastically.

I could tell, being an intuitive person, that Dylan wanted some alone time with Shona to say goodbye to his oldest friend before we disappeared into the wide blue yonder. He shot me a grateful look when I announced that they should go and do the Bureau de Change stuff because they were good with figures, leaving Paul and Grace to help me make an all important decision between a fry-up (lots of protein, less carbs) and a continental breakfast (less protein, lots of carbs).

The three of us grabbed a table and I reached into my backpack.

'Hey, guitar girl,' I said to Grace. 'I got you a present.' I handed her a little box I'd plastered in anime stickers.

Grace beamed. 'Ooooh, I love presents,' she

squealed excitedly, opening the lid. Then her lip started wobbling. Paul peered over her shoulder.

'What is all that crap in there?' he asked, raising an eyebrow.

I punched him on the shoulder. 'There's my lucky plectrum and my lucky magic marker that I used to write our set lists with and my lucky Hello Kitty hairslide that I wore when we played our first gig and . . .'

'Oh and your lucky piece of material that you kissed before you went on stage,' finished Grace.

'It's probably from one of Courtney Love's dresses,' I explained to Paul, who snorted, opened his mouth to say something really crushing and then thought better of it.

'I'm not going to go there,' he decided.

'Best not to,' I agreed. 'So how's Poppy?' I added as an afterthought because I hadn't been able to get her red, angry face out of my mind. 'Still mad at me?'

Grace looked uncomfortable. 'Well, she has deep emotional problems.'

'That doesn't really answer the question,' I muttered, taking a sip of the most disgusting cappuccino in the world.

'She doesn't understand why you don't fancy the idea of being one of her sidekicks on the route to stardom,' Grace finished angrily.

I looked at her in surprise. 'Is she still giving you a hard time about learning the songs?'

'She's giving me a hard time about everything,' Grace complained. 'I wish I had the chance to be the eldest . . . And as for Jack . . . he's started spending all his time with Jesse, who is a totally bad influence on him. He's become all flippant.'

There was obviously trouble in Grace and Jack's wiggy version of paradise but once Grace got onto the subject of her and Jack, I just didn't have the energy.

'Look why don't you email me while I'm away,' I suggested. 'It's *cutiesnowgirl@hotmail.com*. I'm going to be checking my mail whenever I can find free wifi.'

'Cutiesnowgirl?' Grace spluttered.

I glared at her. 'What? It's a cool address.'

'Whatever!'

I definitely liked Grace better when she was too scared to even say hello to me.

Check-in was torturous. It was all 'Who packed your suitcase?' and 'Did anyone give you a package to take on to the plane?' I mean, duh! Dylan, in particular, was given a good old grilling. I guess his torn jeans, Powerpuffs T-shirt (an ironic statement, apparently) and haircut with nail scissors was never going to get us upgraded to first class.

Saying goodbye to Shona and Paul and Grace was horrible. Shona alternated between murmuring endearments about how much she was going to miss us and dire warnings about drive-by shootings and the dangerous additives they put in American food.

We loitered by Passport Control, trying to say goodbye but not really getting anywhere until Dylan grabbed his bag with one hand and me with the other.

'We're going,' he said firmly. 'They're about to call our flight and Edie reckons she can get a sizeable shopping hit in the Duty Free.'

'So this is goodbye then,' Shona sniffed. She hugged us fiercely and started walking away. I knew she was crying, the sappy cow. Grace looked like she was about to seriously lose it too. I flung my arms round her and took deep breaths of her scent: vanilla perfume and fabric softener and Hubba Bubba.

'Go on, get out of here,' I muttered, giving her a little push and she gave a sob and rushed after Shona.

Two down, one to go. Paul shifted from foot to foot and then gave us a little wave before rushing after Shona.

Going away would be all right if it wasn't for the goodbyes.

New York

I'll spare you the details of Duty Free (but there were big savings to be made on all Clinique products) and I'll gloss over most of the flight. Let's just say that neither Dylan or me travel well. I was OK until the engine roared into life as we raced down the runway. But the moment the plane shuddered into the air and the only thing that seemed to keep it up was my blind and shaky belief in aeronautical engineering, I suddenly regretted the bacon butty I'd had earlier.

Dylan was just as bad. We spent most of the flight gripping hands and concentrating on keeping the plane in the air. That, and worrying that we were going to contract deep vein thrombosis if we didn't get up every half hour to stretch our legs.

I don't think Colin, the plastics salesman who was sitting next to Dylan, appreciated my little nuggets of in-flight information. Especially when I reminded Dylan that the pressure in the cabin made the air Sahara Desert-dry and we needed to drink a litre of water for every hour that we were airborne.

By the time the plane landed with a graceful lurch Dylan and I were exhausted.

'Your skin is the weirdest shade of grey,' Dylan muttered to me as we waited in the longest queue in the world to get through Immigration. 'And your hair's standing on end. We are *so* going to get our cases searched.'

Well, we didn't. Instead we took the dinky airport bus to the subway station and got on the train to downtown Manhattan. The minute we sat down, Dylan put his head on my shoulder and promptly fell asleep. I fretted that our suitcases made us look like a pair of tourists who'd just stepped off a plane (well actually, yeah!) and that we might just as well have had a sign printed that read: 'Please beat us up and steal all our money.'

Except no-one paid us the slightest bit of attention and as I watched the funny-shaped houses with their verandas and screen doors whizz past and heard the driver announce place names like Rockaway Boulevard and Euclid Avenue, I suddenly realised that I was in America! Home of every movie and TV show that I'd ever loved. Where people say, 'Have a nice day' and look like they mean it. I was sitting on a subway train surrounded by New Yorkers. I half wanted to break into a rousing song: '*If I can make it there, I'll make it anywhere . . .*' but I managed to restrain myself.

I nudged Dylan but he didn't stir. 'Hey D, we made it,' I whispered and kissed the top of his head.

Building your city on a grid system seems like a logical thing to do until you realise that people from Manchester, England have no idea which way east, west, north or south is. Dylan was no help, though he got very excited when he finally came to, which was about the same time as I tried to negotiate him and our luggage up the subway station steps.

'St Mark's Place,' he gushed. I didn't even know Dylan could gush. 'Andy Warhol has walked down this street!'

Lewis's brother and girlfriend lived in an apartment building on Sixth Street between 1st and 2nd Avenues. They weren't in but their room-mate (US term for flatmate) grudgingly let us in to the tiniest apartment I've ever been in. It was smaller than my bedroom back home.

Ed (the roomie) grunted at us and went back to playing on the X-Box and Dylan and I stood awkwardly in the middle of the room, which was dwarfed by a double bed and the biggest TV this side of a cinema screen.

'Where are we going to sleep?' I hissed at Dylan, who shrugged helplessly.

Eventually Ed was persuaded to budge up and make room for us on the couch and Dylan tried to bond with him over the WWF game he was playing. But when Carl and Lisa turned up it soon became clear that although we were all talking English we weren't speaking the same language and I don't mean saying 'sidewalk' instead of 'pavement'.

They'd barely said hello before taking us down to look at the car. And I use the word 'car' in its loosest possible sense. Anyone who called it a wreck held together with plaster and sticky tape wouldn't be accused of exaggeration.

'It handles like a dream,' Carl was saying as Dylan and I looked at each other with dawning expressions of dismay, disappointment, disgust and many other words beginning with d.

'Well, you like vintage things, don't you?' Dylan said to me finally, before turning to Carl and Lisa and asking them lots of questions about insurance and MOTs and road fund licences, none of which they appeared to understand. They were too busy cracking up over 'your funny accents'.

Dylan and Carl decided to take the car for a spin round the block so we could be sure that the thing actually worked and I trooped upstairs with Lisa who reckoned she might have some English Breakfast Tea tucked away somewhere.

'So, um, the apartment's really small,' I said hesitantly. 'Are you sure there's going to be room for me and Dylan?'

She flicked her long blonde hair out of her eyes and looked at me as if I'd asked if I could murder her firstborn. Lisa was one of those people who it's impossible to feel at ease with. She was thin, dieted-to-the-bone thin rather than fast-metabolism-thin and wearing a business suit with trainers.

'Well, don't you wanna, y'know, get going?' she asked with a slight edge to her voice.

Oh where was D when I needed him? 'Well, it's just that we've been up for eighteen hours with the flight and everything and Lewis said we'd be OK to crash . . .'

'Lewis had no right to say that,' she interrupted me, getting all assertive and hard-faced like those lady lawyers in courtroom thrillers. 'And we need to talk about how much you're going to pay for the loan of the car.'

I blinked once, twice, three times. 'Pay?'

She turned her icy-blue gaze onto me. 'Well, yeah!'

'No,' I said firmly. 'Lewis said we'd be doing you a favour. You need to get the car to LA, we're going to drive it there. No-one said anything about paying.'

'Look, if you were doing a fly-drive you'd have to pay, like, $300 a week for the car,' Lisa insisted. 'So Carl and I were thinking, y'know, you could give us a lump sum of $1000 and you get ten weeks to drive to LA and you save, like, loads of money.'

There was still no sign of Dylan. 'Hang on, you can't

just suddenly decide you want money when it's already been discussed . . .' I trailed off.

Lisa raised her eyebrows. 'Take it or leave it.'

'$500.'

'$950.'

I glared at her. 'I'm not paying more than $600.'

She glared back. '$650.'

Still no sign of Dylan. I was going to have to make an executive decision. 'Final offer. $625.'

She considered it for a minute. 'OK, $625 plus the Clinique perfume you bought in Duty Free.'

'Done,' I said weakly, hoping Dylan was going to be OK about this.

Usually I left the executive decision-making to him. Hell, usually I left it to Grace if it meant that I didn't have to shoulder the burden of responsibility.

'How much?!' Dylan shouted at me.

It was much, much later on. Carl and Dylan had come back from their ride around the block all matey in that strange way that boys do within five minutes of meeting each other. They'd already decided that the apartment was too small and that there was a cheap hotel a couple of blocks along (please note new familiarity with US lingo) where we could stay. I thought they'd already talked money, which goes to show how little I know. I was sure Dylan was going to be dead impressed at my haggling skills as

I mentioned the small sum of $625 I'd shelled out.

'Why are you shouting at me?' I shouted back as I closed the door of our hotel room and dropped my suitcase on the floor. 'They wanted $1000! You should be thanking me.'

'$625!' Dylan screamed. I'd never heard his voice go that high before.

'That's almost £500 which you didn't need to give her.'

'They'd obviously already agreed that she was going to do the money side of it while you two bonded over the fuel injection,' I snapped venomously.

'Oh don't start,' said Dylan warningly. 'Don't try and make this my fault. I already talked to Carl and offered to take him and Lisa out to dinner tomorrow night to say thanks. Oh, but no, you have to give them half our money . . .'

Dylan was ranting now. Nostrils flared, fists clenched, every muscle in his body taut with barely suppressed rage. I watched his mouth open and close as he banged on about my irresponsible behaviour.

'. . . and we have to fork out for this crummy hotel room. And we're right outside the lift so that's going to be making noise all night . . . Where are you going?'

I didn't bother answering as I slammed the bathroom door shut behind me and locked it. I was cold, dirty, tired, hungry and couldn't cope with the shouty jerk who was inhabiting Dylan's body.

I heard him shout, 'Typical' and kick one of the suitcases over before I started running a bath.

17th July (still New York)

We still weren't talking the next morning. I'd been so pissed off with Dylan that when I came out of the bathroom I hadn't let him share the last of Mum's sarnies and he'd had to go to bed hungry. For the first time ever we'd slept with six inches of bed between us but when I woke up we were doing our usual conjoined twins impersonation. Dylan had an arm around my waist and one of his legs curled around mine. But we still weren't talking unless you count muttered one-liners about going down for breakfast and who had the guidebook as conversation.

We finally emerged from the hotel at ten thirty and nothing could prepare me for the humidity of New York in mid July. Flying always leaves me feeling cold and clammy so I hadn't noticed it yesterday but today I felt like I was stepping into a hot, wet, smelly fog and within seconds sweat was dripping down my face. I must have looked like a hunk of red, sweaty cheese. I took off my cardigan and stuffed it into my Cath Kidston messenger bag.

Dylan gave me a considered look. 'What do you want to do today?' he asked finally.

I shrugged. 'I don't know. What do you want to do?' I knew exactly what he wanted to do: a couple of art exhibitions and a trip to some trendy minimalist artboy shop to buy T-shirts but he wasn't playing.

'No, I asked what you wanted to do,' he hissed belligerently.

'Don't try and pick another fight with me,' I snarled, fronting up to him. 'You go and do whatever it is you want to do and I'll see you later.'

And with that I flounced off. If ever I was on *Mastermind*, then flouncing would be my specialist subject. And as an added bonus, I know it really pisses him off. I flounced as far as the deli that was two doors down, which is basically a fancy US corner-shop with a cold meat counter and fresh fruit salad in tubs and was counting out all the weirdy coinage to pay for my bottle of water when Dylan caught up with me.

He stood at the counter while I counted out dimes and nickels and tried to remember what each one was worth.

He still didn't say anything while I rummaged in my bag for my sunglasses and sunblock. It was a little unnerving. All of a sudden he swooped down and kissed me gently on the lips.

'Sorry,' we both said in unison.

I held out my little finger. 'Friends?' I said in a tiny voice.

He gravely hooked my little finger with his. 'Friends.'

'Look, about the money—' I began.

Dylan shook his head. 'Forget it, I overreacted. They probably planned the whole thing. It's only £500, we have plenty of money.'

I nudged him with my hip. 'I should have waited for you.' I looked up at him. I've known Dylan forever, or nearly three years anyway, and even now all I have to do is look at him to get quite giddy with longing. Dylan is all angles; long limbs and sharp features softened slightly by his terminally messy dark brown hair, and the audacious curve of his bottom lip. Right now he was looking at me with a small smile, his hands shielding his green eyes from the sun so I couldn't read his expression. He could make me do anything sometimes just by looking at me in a certain way. Pretty much the way he was looking at me right now.

'So . . . c'mon, I know you want to go to the Guggenheim and admire its unique rotunda architectural feature as designed by Frank Lloyd Wright,' I said.

Dylan grinned then boffed me lightly on the nose. 'You can read me like a book.'

'Yeah – a cheap airport novel,' I mock-sneered. 'Let's find the subway station.'

We spent the morning getting lost on the subway and looking at art. It was all very cultural. But the best thing was getting our lunchtime hot dogs and pretzels from one of those street carts they always have in the movies. Dylan and I were back to being love-shaped although the air was far too sticky to even think about holding hands.

We made our way back downtown in the afternoon so Dylan could stock up on art boy T-shirts but there's only so many skate shops a girl can visit.

'You carry on,' I told Dylan as we made our fourth shop stop. 'I'm going to pop into that café and check my emails.'

As I suspected there was an email from Grace waiting in my in-box.

To: cutiesnowgirl@hotmail.com
From: graceofmyheart@hotmail.com

Hey Edie

Hope you're OK and if you're reading this then I guess you haven't been sprayed wid gunshot. It's all kicked off here. There I was, all excited about going on tour until I found out . . . (dramatic pause) Jack's coming too! No, he hasn't had a sex change and persuaded Poppy to let him play the triangle. He's going to be our roadie. And it's all Jesse's fault. They have this whole Batman and Robin thing going on – it's very trying. I used to think that I stood a chance with Jack but it's like he's obsessed with Jesse. I mean, Poppy goes out with the

guy and gives him a hard time about everything so I
don't see why Jack's gone down with such a bad case
of hero worship.

Oh grumble, grumble.

Anyway gotta go. Write soon.

Gracie xxxxx

I shook my head. It was so easy to see where Grace was
going wrong with her life. Much easier than sussing
out my own problem areas. I clicked on the reply
button.

To: graceofmyheart@hotmail.com
From: cutiesnowgirl@hotmail.com

Hey Grace

Greetings from NYC. We're both still in one piece
although Dylan's disappeared into yet another shop
that sells skinny T-shirts with interesting graphics on
them.

We've had some jet-lag induced domestics over the
last few hours (long, complicated story) but we just
need more sleep and food and everything will be fine.

Anyway I'm going to use the excuse of jet-lag to do
some straight talking. I know you fancy Jack (don't give
me that look) so the fact that he's going to be on tour
gives you the perfect chance to do something about it!
Just grab him and snog him! Dylan's leaning over my

shoulder and reading this. He says hi and that we have to go now. My 'master' has spoken and I'm powerless to resist. (Yup, those were sarcastic quote marks!)

Take care

Edie xxxxx

Dylan rubbed my shoulders as I closed my in-box.

'Are you tired?' he wanted to know.

I nodded. 'Yeah, shall we have extra caffeine-y coffee or a nap?'

'A nap,' decided Dylan immediately. 'And I can't be bothered to faff about with the subway, let's get a cab.'

It sounded like a plan. A good plan.

Half an hour later we were fast asleep.

I woke up to find Dylan kissing my ear and stroking my hair. I lay there for five minutes pretending to be asleep because it felt so nice. But then Dylan pressed himself against my back and slid his hand lower.

'I know you're not asleep,' he purred. 'Your breathing's got faster.'

I smiled and rolled over so I was lying on top of him.

I brushed the hair out of his eyes. 'Hey you,' I whispered.

'Hey yourself,' he whispered back before nibbling my bottom lip with his teeth. I rubbed my mouth against his but every time he tried to capture my lips I moved away, kissing his cheeks and eyelids and the tip of his nose. Dylan gave a growl of annoyance and suddenly flipped me so I was lying underneath him while his mouth clung to mine. Our lips met, Dylan's tongue dipping into my mouth as our legs slowly tangled.

Eventually he paused in his assault of my mouth and I sucked in some much needed oxygen.

'What time are we meeting Carl and Lisa?' Dylan mumbled, in between kissing my neck.

I tried to think. 'Eight.'

Dylan glanced at the travel clock on his bedside table. 'We've got two hours.'

I ran my hands down his back, feeling the tight outline of his muscles beneath the skin.

'I guess I could have a long soak in the bath,' I suggested teasingly. 'That should kill some time.'

Dylan nipped my shoulder. 'Why don't you make it a quick shower instead, I've got plans for you.'

The evening air was a little fresher as we walked through Soho towards Nolita, stopping every now and then to consult our street map. After a few false turns we found Mulberry Street and the little Italian restaurant where we'd arranged to meet Carl and Lisa. I was a bit nervous about hanging out with them. Lisa hadn't exactly endeared herself to me and Carl was probably the biggest jerk in the world if his choice in girlfriend was anything to go by. But they seemed pleased to see us, probably 'cause they were getting a free meal. God, I've become so cynical in my old age.

We sat outside and watched these little old Italian men greeting each other and sitting down outside a café a few doors down to smoke cigars and drink red wine. Carl swore to God that the whole block was Mafia controlled and that they were retired members of the Cosa Nostra but I think he'd seen too many episodes of *The Sopranos*. I was in love with it all. The waitress with the broad Bronx accent who made me repeat my order for spaghetti and meatballs five times because 'I love your cute accent', the smell of garlic and traffic, the thick, heavy air and the fact that every other person I saw was walking a small dog.

Carl and Lisa didn't talk about the stuff our friends in Manchester talked about: mainly who fancied who, who hated who and music, films and art. They talked about their sinus problems, how expensive living in New York was and gave a really in-depth account of the state of their relationship (which veered dangerously towards over-sharing). After a long, tedious account about Carl's bad relationship with his stepfather which had started when he'd walked in on him and his mum getting pelvic, I changed the subject to ask how much rent they paid.

Carl squinched his face at me. 'I think that's a really personal question and I'm kinda offended that you'd ask me that,' he said very haughtily.

I apologised and looked at Dylan for a bit of moral support but he was too busy talking to Lisa about her therapist.

I couldn't wait for the meal to be over and wondered whether Dylan and I would have time for a romantic walk in Central Park but once we'd settled the bill, Carl and Lisa were already making plans to take us bar-hopping.

'Edie's underage,' Dylan pointed out. 'Don't you have to be twenty-one to drink here?'

Carl winked at me, which threw me as he hadn't exactly been Mr New Best Friend up till then and promised we'd go somewhere dark where I wouldn't get carded.

Then Dylan and Lisa were walking on ahead while Carl slung a slightly too friendly arm round my shoulders and started jawing on about his and Lisa's sex life. It was too ewwww for words. There was something off, something that I couldn't quite put my finger on but Carl was following Dylan and Lisa through a little doorway and my feeling of ickiness got distracted.

The Red Bench Bar was so dark that if Carl hadn't moved his arm from my shoulder to my waist and guided me towards a table I'd have had to ask the barman for some night-vision goggles.

While Dylan and Carl went to the bar Lisa and I sat in silence as we acclimatised to the dark. She twirled a strand of her expensively highlighted hair around one perfectly manicured finger and even though I was wearing my expensive Mango dress that looked a bit like a Marc Jacobs frock, I felt like a raggedy urchin next to her.

'Dylan's cute,' Lisa suddenly announced. 'Extremely yummy.'

'He'll do,' I said in a non-committal voice that I hoped made it clear that Dylan's yumminess was not up for discussion.

'You still mad about the money, huh?' she asked and although it was dark, I could hear the smirk in her voice. 'I explained it to Dylan, he's cool with it.'

'Well he wasn't cool about it last night,' I muttered.

'You gotta know how to handle men, honey,' Lisa said with all the added and vast experience of her extra four years on me. 'Take Carl.'

Yeah, someone, please take Carl.

I sighed. 'What about Carl?'

'He's OK for now, but definitely not a long-term fixture.' Lisa shifted nearer to me as she warmed to her topic. 'It's like you and Dylan.'

'It's nothing like me and Dylan,' I burst out indignantly. 'We love each other!'

But when I said it, it sounded, well, trite. Lisa seemed to agree.

'God, you teenagers figure that love is always going to be all puppy dogs and ice cream,' she snorted dismissively. 'He's your first boyfriend, of course you think you love him. But when you go to college all that stuff changes.'

'It doesn't have to,' I argued. 'If two people love each other then they can make it work.'

Lisa ignored this. 'Carl and I have an open relationship,' she continued. 'It makes everything less complicated. I'm so pleased that I've moved on from all that jealousy 'cause, y'know, that negative energy can be so blocking.'

'Open relationships are just an excuse to cheat on each other,' I snorted.

'Don't you ever think about being with someone who isn't Dylan?' Lisa demanded in a low voice. 'I know Carl really likes you.'

'Yeah?'

'No I mean he *really* likes you,' Lisa giggled. 'And I know Dylan's into me.'

My entire brain was on the verge of exploding, when Carl and Dylan came back with our drinks. Carl was already sliding into the booth next to me and Lisa was patting the seat next to her for Dylan, who had no choice but to sit down. He didn't have to look so bloody happy about it, though.

Then Carl put his hand on my knee under the table and whispered, 'So. Did Lisa talk to you?'

My withering glance was annoyingly obscured so I took a gulp of my drink, and nearly spat it out again.

The three of them laughed at me, and Lisa made a big show of mopping the table with her napkin. 'Oh yeah, forgot to mention how large the measures are,' Dylan grinned.

'Thanks for the warning,' I said sourly.

And then Carl was telling me how many bench presses he could do and while I idly wondered what a bench press was and wished that he'd stop trying to look down my dress, I tried to hear what Dylan and Lisa were talking about. I heard my name mentioned a few times, and I didn't like the way Lisa kept gazing into Dylan's eyes and licking her lips.

For the next two hours, Carl kept the drinks coming in between trying to touch me in inappropriate places. I attempted to kick Dylan under the table a few times but he was too engrossed in Lisa to notice. He'd occasionally flash me a quick smile and then turn back to her.

I realised eventually that I was really drunk. I had to fight the urge to lay my head down on the table. Carl was now wittering on about how my accent was really horny and rubbing my thigh and it was getting harder and harder to keep hold of his hand to stop it wandering someplace that it really shouldn't be wandering.

'Oh look, they're holding hands. That's so cute.'

I tried to focus on Lisa who'd just spoken but there was at least three of her.

'I feel a bit strange,' I said slowly, my voice coming from a long, long way away.

Dylan stood up. 'Jesus, Edie, I can't take you anywhere,' he snapped.

I tried to stand too but realised I was still clutching Carl's hand.

'Are we going?' I asked the three Dylans who were looking at me with matching expressions of disgust.

Carl gave me an enthusiastic hug. 'Hey, you can't go!' he exclaimed loudly. 'The party's just getting started.'

But Carl's squeezing was having a devastating effect on my insides. 'I'm going to be sick!'

With an exasperated exhalation, Dylan grabbed me by the arm and dragged me through the bar. Somewhere in my brain, I'd already made the decision that I was going to throw up and didn't feel all panicky about it like you do when you're ill. I stumbled to the edge of the kerb and puked. And puked. And puked. When my stomach was empty, I felt a lot better and strangely calm. I turned round; Dylan was staring at me with a look of utter revulsion, his arms folded.

I stepped back, bewildered by the venom in his eyes, and nearly fell off the edge of the sidewalk. In two short strides he was clutching my arm again. 'You've made a complete show of yourself,' he spat, his green eyes flashing, as he turned me round to face him. 'You just shouldn't drink.'

'Leggo of me,' I slurred. 'You're not the boss of me. I'm going back in and I'm having another drink.'

'You've had enough,' Dylan said tightly. 'Of drinking, and all that touchy feely crap with Carl.'

At that moment Carl and Lisa emerged from the bar, took one look at the thunderous expression on Dylan's face and stopped.

'I'm taking Edie back to the hotel,' Dylan stated in an expressionless voice, which I knew meant that I was for it when he got me on my own. However much I was beginning to loathe our new American pals, I decided there was safety in numbers.

'I want to go with them,' I whined.

Dylan kept up the death grip on my upper arms.

'It's been a great night,' he said to Carl and Lisa, ignoring my frantic wriggling. 'We'll phone you when we get to LA, let you know the car's in one piece.'

They realised they were being dismissed and turned to go but Dylan hadn't finished.

'Oh, and Lisa,' he said in his scary, quiet voice that always sends shivers down my spine. And not in a good way. 'Can I have the $600 back?'

Lisa opened and shut her mouth a couple of times.

'Yeah what was all that about?' Carl said to her. 'Why should they pay for doing us a favour?' He turned to Dylan. 'It's like I told you, we'd have had to pay a fortune to get the car shipped back to LA.'

Lisa was digging furiously in her purse. 'There's $500,' she hissed at Dylan, slamming a wodge of bills into his hand. 'I don't have the rest.'

Carl threw her a mean look and she raised her eyebrows at him before he drew out a crumpled $100 bill from his jacket pocket. 'There you go, man, sorry about that.' He lowered his voice. 'Chicks, huh?' And Carl and Lisa exited stage left.

Dylan let go of me and I staggered backwards.

'I wasn't doing anything with him, I mean . . .'

Dylan made a dismissive face. 'I don't want to hear it, Edie,' he said tiredly, shoving his hands into his hip pockets. 'I just want to go back to the hotel and forget that this last half hour ever happened.'

'Dylan, I . . .' I didn't finish the sentence. Dylan was already standing in the road, trying to flag down a cab and not paying any attention to me.

I got into the cab which had just pulled up, went back to the hotel and for the second night running, Dylan and I weren't talking.

18th July (still New York)

Dylan was still mad at me the next day. He didn't say he was mad (he didn't say much of anything) but had made an unnecessarily harsh decision to check out early. Eight in the morning, early. All I wanted to do was burrow under the covers and wonder if some small animal had crawled into my mouth during the night and died.

Hangovers are not of the good. Even the merest twitch of an eyelash made my head thump and my stomach lurch but Dylan ignored my muffled protests and went down to breakfast after tersely informing me that he wanted me washed, packed and ready to go in half an hour. The slamming of the door was an added Dylan bonus.

By eight thirty-five I was clutching a triple shot espresso from the nearest Starbucks as I stood meekly watching Dylan load up the car and swearing under his breath. I tried to lift my suitcase and show willing but he snatched it from me and told me to get in the car. Never come between a boy and his bad mood.

The wreck had one long seat up front and I carefully arranged my maps and the itinerary notebook and my bag in the middle so no part of me could touch any part of Dylan. That took all of thirty seconds but Dylan was still faffing about.

I didn't know what was taking him so long. We had two suitcases plus assorted carrier bags and a whole boot and back seat to put them on.

Eventually he was done packing and slid into the driver's seat.

Dylan put the key in the ignition, checked the rear-view mirror, adjusted his seat, wound down the window, wound it up again when he realised that it was hotter outside than it was inside the car, then put his hands on the steering wheel and gave a deep sigh.

There wasn't a lot I could do. He was obviously nervous about driving a clapped out heap of junk and on the wrong side of the road but anything I said was going to sound majorly unsupportive given the foul mood he was in. I contented myself by slowly stretching my facial muscles into a bright smile which I'm sure would have been very encouraging if Dylan could have forced himself to look at me.

We sat there for another couple of minutes before Dylan suddenly turned the key and the engine roared into life. Dylan looked a bit surprised, recovered himself and gently eased away from the kerb.

We were on our way.

Two hours later I was still plucking up the courage to talk to Dylan. Even if it was to ask him to stop at the nearest place that sold food so I could try solids and see if they stayed down. He'd worked through his driving demons and was now relaxed. His shades were on, his arm resting on the edge of the open window but every time I shifted on the seat or made a move to turn down the volume on the Arcade Fire mix he was playing, he'd shoot me a look that was equal parts distaste and equal parts reproach.

I was having a hard time remembering why Dylan was still so angry with me. Yes, I'd got drunk and made a total fool of myself but he'd been the one who'd left me to the evil clutches of Carl while he was engrossed with Lisa.

'Dylan?'

'What?' he replied curtly.

I took a deep breath and counted to ten. 'How long are you planning on giving me the silent treatment?'

'I haven't decided.'

'I got drunk, I threw up. Like, you haven't done that a hundred times!' I pointed out.

'I don't hold hands with people while you're sitting opposite me,' snapped Dylan, unable to maintain the ironic detached thing.

'D, that guy had been groping me for hours but you were so occupied with Lisa, you didn't notice,' I pleaded. 'I was holding his hand because it was the only way to stop it heading straight for . . . well, y'know.'

'Whatever.'

'You don't believe me?'

Dylan changed lanes, the car juddering slightly with the aggressive movement.

'I believe you,' he sighed.

'You want to try that once more, with feeling?' I mused.

'OK. I do believe you,' insisted Dylan with a bit more vehemence. 'But I am not spending the whole trip cleaning up your mess. I don't see why I always have to be the designated adult.'

We exchanged a look. Dylan's mouth was set in a stern line; I searched intently for some sign that he was softening towards me. There wasn't one. I touched his leg gently. 'Dylan, I'm sorry,' I said with every ounce of sincerity I had. 'I don't know what else I can say. I'm sorry for all of it.'

Dylan arched his eyebrow as if to say, 'go on'.

I slid nearer to him. 'C'mon, let this be the real start of our holiday. Let's put New York behind us.'

I reached over and kissed him on the cheek. Still no reaction. I stuck out my tongue and slowly licked his neck before nibbling on his earlobe in a way that I knew made him come over all unnecessary and he snaked his arm round my waist so I couldn't move away.

'OK,' he all but purred. 'I forgive you. New start.'

'I hate arguing with you,' I said plaintively. 'And that's all we seem to have been doing ever since we got here.'

'Jet lag,' decided Dylan. 'And for the record, I *was* engrossed with Lisa.'

My heart sank. 'You were?'

'Yeah, because she was . . . so weird,' Dylan tried to grope for the right word. 'Not interesting weird. Scary weird. Like, she was completely self-obsessed but she called it "being tuned in to her inner being". For a while I thought she was coming on to me.'

'She *was* coming on to you,' I said indignantly. 'She said that she and Carl have an "open relationship".'

'Oh, right,' said Dylan a bit nonplussed. He was silent for a few seconds. 'God, she *really* was weird.'

It took us a day to drive to Philadelphia and what can I tell you? The journey was like being in an arthouse film. Like when they show you all those different shots to mark a passage of time and you know the hero and the heroine are crazy in love with each other and everything's sun-dappled. It was exactly like that.

We sang along with the Elvis compilation that Italian Tony at the café had made us as a going-away present. And we stopped at an authentic American diner for lunch, where Dylan's waffles and ham (just focus on the ham part of the lunch) came with icing sugar smothered over the top and a bottle of maple syrup that he was expected to pour liberally over his plate. And once we were back in the wreck I kicked off my Birkenstocks and rested my feet on the dashboard and stared out at the yellow school buses and the big square cars with their tinted windows and 'New Jersey – The Garden State' number plates.

Philadelphia

It was mid-afternoon as we crossed over the Delaware River into Philadelphia. I juggled the outsize map from one of the guidebooks and directed Dylan towards the city centre or 'center' as the Americans insist on spelling it.

Dylan gave a low whistle. 'Dead impressed with the map-reading, Eeds.'

I pulled a face. 'We used to go caravanning to France every year and not only did I have to navigate but I had to do it in French!' I winced at the memory.

After a few 'umms' and 'maybes' we pulled into the driveway of a motel whose sign Dylan didn't actively hate and went to check in. There was a little awkward moment when the man at the desk thought I was underage and demanded to see some ID while Dylan spluttered, 'She's nineteen, look at her passport!' but after slapping down a room deposit we had cabin 31 for the next two nights.

Dylan stretched and groaned as I opened the curtains and let the afternoon sun flood through the room.

'You all driven out, D?' I asked as I went into the bathroom to see if the free toiletries were up to much. They so weren't.

'I'm a bit stiff,' came Dylan's muffled reply as he collapsed onto the bed.

'I've got some tiger balm somewhere,' I said vaguely. 'We could go for a walk and get something to eat.'

Dylan stretched again before staggering to his feet and pulling his T-shirt over his head. He rubbed his neck tiredly.

I caught sight of ourselves in the mirror. Dylan looked so beautiful. Not many boys are beautiful but Dylan is. Some people would say that he is too bony but I love his leanness. The way all of him is taut, no matter how many plates of pasta he devours in an attempt to bulk up. And I love the slightly crooked angle of his nose and the way his cheekbones are so sharply defined and that his left eyebrow is constantly quirking upwards. I am less beautiful. Dylan always tells me I'll age into beauty when I'm moaning about my freckles and the way my mouth is too large. Sometimes I think I look like an alien with my big eyes and pointed chin, and nose that almost isn't there. Maybe my fringe is too short. I tugged on my ponytail and frowned, suddenly realising that Dylan had disappeared and by the sounds coming from the bathroom was power showering.

* * *

Dylan emerged half an hour later with a towel wrapped round his hips. He looked squeaky clean but dog tired.

'It'll be dark soon,' I said, figuring that any sight-seeing could wait till tomorrow. 'Why don't I get us something to eat and we can watch a movie or something on the TV? I think there's a film channel.'

Dylan gave me a slightly surprised look but nodded in agreement.

'Will you be OK going out on your own?'

I nodded. 'Yeah, I'll be half an hour. Tops.'

When I got back with sandwiches the size of concrete breeze-blocks and a carton of Ben & Jerry's, Dylan was fast asleep. I contemplated waking him but he looked so peaceful that I took my turkey bagel and the ice cream and sat on the bench outside and watched the stars while I ate.

19th July

Philadelphia is the birthplace of democracy. That was my reason for insisting that Dylan came with me to see the Liberty Bell but he was less than impressed.

'It's got a big crack in it,' he pointed out. 'And it's slightly unpatriotic of you to make me look at stuff that commemorates the English getting their butts kicked.'

'But, it's history,' I squeaked, scandalised.

Dylan looked unimpressed. 'Can we go to the Rodin Museum now?'

'Whatever.' I plucked at my pink checked shirt. It was so hot. Maybe jeans hadn't been such a good idea.

Dylan perked up when we got to the museum, although he'd been pretty chipper after his fourteen-hour sleep marathon. Apparently he'd woken up at two in the morning, scarfed down the sandwich I'd put on his bedside table before I got into bed and then fell asleep for another six hours.

The museum was air-conditioned which made me happy and there was plenty of sculpture which made Dylan happy. Dylan really knows the drill when it comes to art. He can look at a painting or a sculpture for ages and I never know if he's wigging on the art or just being a great big ponce. Me? I just look at something, decide whether I like it or not and then I'm good to go. We spent four hours in that museum. Four hours of my life that I'm never getting back. Grrrr.

Washington

20th July

We're back on the road. According to my never wrong itinerary it's a 139 mile drive to Washington which is just about bearable considering it's boiling hot in the car. I'd never really given a moment's thought to air conditioning before but with my thighs sticking to the leather seat and the sun glaring in through the windscreen it's all that I can think about.

Well, not the only thing. I'm thinking about Dylan a lot. About how spending all this time with just him is starting to drive me a little crazy. Every time I turn my head, he's there. And I'm comfortable with him but I don't want to be too comfortable with him. I need to have my mystery and that means that I don't want him trying to clean his teeth while I'm having a shower. That was the first thing we rowed about this morning.

He'd sauntered into the bathroom without a care in the world and seemed completely surprised when

I'd screamed and wrapped the shower curtain around me.

'Get out!' I'd squeaked.

Dylan just couldn't understand why I'd got so mad. How standing butt-naked in a shower made me feel more vulnerable than when we were getting, well, pelvic.

'It's nothing I haven't seen before,' he'd leered before I'd thrown a shampoo bottle at him and he'd realised I was serious.

By the time I'd come out of the bathroom fully clothed, Dylan had realised I had nudity issues and apologised but now we were stuck in the car again and it was hot and we were both acting like gritty toddlers. I mean we'd argued over everything; from what tape to play, why I had to have two cups of coffee when I know they make me pee to why it was skanky and disgusting to wear the same T-shirt two days running. These weren't major arguments and Dylan kept laughing in the middle of every point he made but it was doing my head in. I'd never realised how confrontational he was. Worse than Poppy. But thinking about Poppy just gave me a big, bad gloom.

Another major US city, another cheap motel room decorated in various shades of beige. Dylan was sitting on the bed, thumbing through the guidebook after changing his T-shirt.

'OK, we can do the National Gallery of Art this afternoon,' he decided. 'Then the National Portrait Gallery tomorrow and maybe the Corcoran.'

'There's more to life than galleries,' I muttered under my breath.

'Yeah. So you hungry?'

I really didn't want another argument. Really, really, really.

'D . . . maybe we should have some alone time tomorrow,' I said hesitantly. ' 'Cause we're arguing a lot and you like the art and I kind of like the art but I also like other things . . .' I tailed off.

Dylan gave me a considered look. I smiled weakly.

'OK,' he said slowly. 'If you're sure you'll be all right on your own?' He sounded as if he thought that was unlikely.

'Of course I will,' I said in a hurt voice. 'I just need to do *me* things. You know, girly things?'

'Look, if you end up dead in a ditch I'll have a hell of a time trying to explain it to your parents,' Dylan announced lightly before promising that we'd only look at twentieth century pop-art this afternoon and absolutely no paintings of naked cherubim from the early sixteenth century.

21st July

To: cutiesnowgirl@hotmail.com
From: graceofmyheart@hotmail.com

It's started! The endless tour rehearsals. Jack has begun his roadie duties already, Jesse's teaching him how to work a PA system and you'd think it was space shuttle command the way they go on about it. But Jack does carry my (well, your) guitar case for me. So I s'pose he's not all bad.

I said hi to Poppy for you but she just said something unrepeatable.

Gotta go! Don't forget about us while you're burning up the freeway.

Love Grace xxx

I took a sip of my drink and sighed. The coffee shop in downtown Washington was a long, long way from Manchester. I mean, I could see the White House from where I was sitting. The people in suits here didn't work in insurance companies, they were like in charge of America, which more or less put them in charge of the world. It made me feel small and insignificant.

I hit 'Reply'.

To: graceofmyheart@hotmail.com
From: cutiesnowgirl@hotmail.com

I love being a girl; a well-read, fashion conscious, heroine-loving girl having an adventure in Washington.

Today I put on my nicest vintage summer frock (the green one with the daisies) and went to Arlington National Cemetery and left some flowers on Jacqueline Kennedy Onassis's grave (because she is one of my all-time top style icons). Then I had a manicure and pedicure (for the bargain price of twenty-five dollars!) and now I'm sipping an iced mochachino and reading your latest email.

Dylan's fine. He's doing the art boy thing today and I'm sure he's secretly relieved that I'm not with him making stupid comments like, 'Picasso was a bit rubbish at drawing hands wasn't he?'

I wish Poppy would stop being mad at me. Maybe she'll start getting over it soon. But don't take any crap from her. You're a great guitarist, you just need to practise more. So go practise!

Missing you

Edie xxx

I admired my newly red-tipped toes as I aimlessly wandered back to the hotel. The weird thing was that spending the day apart from Dylan made me realise how much I noticed when he wasn't there. I was really looking forward to seeing him. And instead of making polite conversation about where we were going to have lunch, I had proper news to tell him, even if it was about putting a bunch of mixed blooms on some dead president's dead wife's grave.

As I walked down the long veranda to our room, I saw Dylan waiting for me. He waved and started walking towards me. He was the most welcoming, exciting thing in this strange place; I couldn't help it. I broke into a run and launched myself at him.

Dylan laughed as he picked me up and swung me round.

'Hey you,' he said teasingly.

I wrapped my arms around his neck and buried my face into his shoulder. He smelt hot and lemony. He smelt like Dylan.

'I missed you,' I said throatily.

Dylan was making no move to put me on my feet and I clung on tighter. He backed me up against the wall and took my mouth in a hot, hungry kiss.

'I. Missed. You,' he breathed in between kisses. He was holding me up with his body and there didn't seem to be a millimetre of him that wasn't pressed against me.

I twined my fingers in his hair as Dylan explored my neck, tracing the pulse that pounded there with the tip of his tongue. It was when I shifted restlessly and wound my legs around him that Dylan gave a groan, and still carrying me, staggered to the open door of our room.

He managed to make it to the bed before letting go of me and then jumped on top of me, making me giggle as he planted slurpy kisses on my shoulders and pushed the straps of my dress out of the way.

'One more minute and we'd have got arrested,' he said.

I rolled over and pinned him down. 'Shut up and kiss me,' I growled.

I think we'd better fade out to black now.

Chicago

1st August

To: <u>graceofmyheart@hotmail.com</u>
From: <u>cutiesnowgirl@hotmail.com</u>

DISCLAIMER: THIS EMAIL IS GOING TO DOUBLE UP AS MY DIARY SO IGNORE ANY OF THE BITS THAT GET TOO INTROSPECTIVE OR BANG ON ABOUT 'FEELINGS'.

Hey you. Sorry I haven't written in ages. You really haven't seen America until you've seen it from the passenger window of a 1993 Chrysler with rust patches that match the bronze paint job and tan leather interior trim.

We've been on the road for a fortnight now. We're into this strange Zen-like rhythm where our entire world is contained inside a car. I was a bit worried about D having to do so much driving but he loves it. He's getting to fulfil all his Jack Kerouac fantasies, although one night we were way behind schedule (the schedule is God!)

and he nearly fell asleep at the wheel. We had to pull over and Dylan had a nap on the back seat while I stayed wide awake and tried to forget about all those stupid urban myths about crazed serial killers with hooks for hands roaming the highways looking for nice, ripe girls and then removing the entrails from their bodies.

So maybe you want to know about the places we've been. I'll try not to make it seem like a boring travelogue.

Gettysburg: Lots of mind-numbing Civil War stuff.

Niagara Falls: Very big waterfall.

Toronto: yup, Toronto, Canada! Good shops and friendly people – with very nasal accents.

Detroit: Or Detroit Rock City, as Dylan insisted on calling it. Lots of car museums.

Chicago: Where we are right now.

In between the big cities we've stopped at little towns just off the freeway. They're all pretty much the same actually. You can't really walk anywhere, because there's just one big main strip, usually with a drive thru Maccy D's, a car showroom and a Pentecostal church. We have discovered Denny's, a fantastic diner chain that's very Fifties looking. It's like Little Chef meets the diner in *Happy Days*. Dylan eats one of their Lumberjack Slam breakfasts every day and they do this Root Beer Float which completely proves, once and for all, that God really does exist! I have to force-feed Dylan fruit while we're in the car otherwise he'd get rickets.

Dylan and I are getting on fine. I didn't really say much before but we were so unfine the first week we were here. Lots of heavy-duty fighting and in-car sniping so I was beginning to wonder if we'd made a big mistake. Twenty-four hours a day in each other's company is a whole new deal. I think we're over the worst of it. Now we feel comfortable again and we can take an hour off in between sentences and it doesn't seem awkward. Or we can spend far too much time pretending to be Iris and Hank, a retired couple from Buttcheek, Illinois who are on their way to a new life in a retirement community just north of Florida. Dylan would kill me if he knew I'd told you that!

More importantly, how are things hanging with you in sunny Manchester? I'm not fooled by your nonchalant talk of Jack, I know you're a seething mass of girl hormones really, so spill! How's Poppy? She must be showing some signs of softening by now. And how many boys have Atsuko and Darby snogged?

I've got to go now. I promised my mum I'd have my photo taken outside the hospital where they used to film *ER*. You think I'm joking? Oh, how I wish I wasn't!
Much love
Edie xxx

I'd just sent Grace's email when my in-box beeped to show there was an incoming message. It was from

Grace. Emails that cross in the ether have to be one of my all-time least favourite things. I glanced over at Dylan who was looking up roadmaps on the internet, even though we had about fifty billion guidebooks and decided I had time to read and reply.

To: cutiesnowgirl@hotmail.com
From: graceofmyheart@hotmail.com

Hey Edie

I hope you're all right and haven't fallen off the edge of the map. I haven't heard from you in ages. We've just got back from playing a one-off gig in Reading. We had to sleep in the van overnight, which I did *not* enjoy. Jack is a pig. I hate him! He's got this stupid new haircut; it's all tufty in the front. It looks ridiculous. And he's bought a pair of skinny jeans and some Adidas Superstars and when we played the gig, girls were looking at him. I don't know why. Probably they were thinking that he looked like an utter dork.

Jesse has a pet name for me, 'Dis-Grace', he says it's because that's what I sound like on guitar. And Poppy just laughed and said that my bedroom should be called Dis-Gracelands. Her and Jesse are moving in together over the café. Mum thinks that he's going to have your old room but I think they're sleeping together. If Poppy picks on me any more I will tell Mum and that'll wipe the smile off Poppy's face.

Atsuko and Darby are nice to me but they spend all their time chasing boys. Were they always like that? They have scorecards and everything.

I'm sort of dreading going away on tour now. I don't think I'm going to learn the songs in time — especially having trouble with the linky bit in 'Fang Boys Suck', could you draw the chords for me and post 'em?

Am going to have a wallowfest with some R Patz DVDs now. Sorry for banging on about all me, me, me but you're the only person who could possibly understand.

Write soon

Grace xxx

PS: Almost forgot. When I woke up from my very uncomfortable sleeping position by the wheel arch, Jack was staring at me really intently. I think I had bed hair. Or van hair. Or something. Creep!

I smirked at the PS. When I was sixteen, I'd spent all my time angsting about my monster-sized crush on Dylan and the vain hope that one day he'd declare his undying love. I looked over at him. He was still mesmerised by his 'puter screen and was now looking at his in-box, even though I was the only one who ever sent him emails. I knew one way of getting his attention.

To: artboy@hotmail.com
From: cutiesnowgirl@hotmail.com

I can't help but wonder if you're the skinny boy with scruffy hair who's sitting near me in a Chicago coffee shop. Wld u lk prv chat?

Beep me baby (one more time!)
From your secret admirer xxx

I grinned as his computer beeped and started to compose my reply to Grace.

To: graceofmyheart@hotmail.com
From: cutiesnowgirl@hotmail.com

Gosh! Could you sound a little more crabby? I guess spending a night hugging a wheel arch will do that to a girl.

So Jack's got a fin and some Superstars? Sounds cool to me. Also sounds as if he's trying to impress a certain girl we both know (er, that'd be you!). You have to be more relaxed about boys or Jack to be more specific. And, Lordy, don't let him know that he's getting to you, just assume a slightly aloof air when he's getting on your nerves and smile mysteriously. Not that I've ever managed to pull that off but I reckon it would work wonders.

Tell Jesse that he has a stupid girl's name next time he calls you *Dis*-Grace and, yeah, of course he and

Poppy are sleeping together. I mean, obvs! But don't tell her that I told you.

    Have to go now. Really have to go.

    I will draw the chords for you and post 'em but it might take a week for you to get them.

Love Edie

PS: Darby and Atsuko have been like that forever!

My wifi time was almost up. Dylan was paying for our coffee as I clicked on the message he'd just sent me.

To: cutiesnowgirl@hotmail.com
From: artboy@hotmail.com

Dear Secret Admirer
Don't get me wrong, I am flattered but I'm already in a loving, committed relationship with a girl who would never ever write anything so lame as 'beep me baby one more time' in an email.
Yours sincerely
Dylan Kowalski (Mr)

We spent most of the day wandering around and going into air-conditioned cafés when the heat got too much. The rest of the time we asked people where Chicago County Hospital was while they looked at us as if we'd asked them if they wanted to accompany us to The Mothership. The things I do for that woman!

2nd August

Last night Dylan didn't sleep at all. His tossing and turning kept waking me up. I thought it was the cold air coming from the ventilator shafts that was stopping him from sleeping. I rolled over so he wouldn't keep disturbing me and went back to this strange dream where I was appearing on the Norwegian version of *Deal or No Deal*.

The first watery rays of sunlight were coming through the blinds when I realised Dylan wasn't in bed. I sat up and stared blearily around the room. He was sitting in a chair in just his boxers, poring over one of the guidebooks.

'Dylan, what are you doing?' I asked sleepily. 'Come back to bed, it's (I peered at the travel clock) five in the morning.'

He turned round. 'Go back to sleep,' he said quietly. 'I just wanted to check something.'

I groaned to let him know he was being weird and snuggled back down. When I next woke up, it was nine and Dylan was asleep in the chair, the top half of him draped over the desk.

I climbed out of bed and ran a gentle hand down his back. I could feel all the individual vertebrae in his spine. Dylan didn't stir.

I crouched down and stroked his hair. 'D,' I whispered in his ear. 'You're gonna have terrible backache when you wake up.'

Dylan muttered something and pushed his head against my hand like a dog does when it's really getting into the whole petting experience. I nudged his shoulder a bit more firmly and Dylan opened his eyes and gingerly sat up.

'Ow, ow, ow,' he moaned as he straightened his spine.

'You should have a shower and put it on sting-spray setting,' I suggested helpfully. 'Then I could give you a massage.'

'Maybe,' Dylan said blearily.

'So what's the deal with you getting up in the middle of the night to start checking the route?' I teased. 'Don't you trust my fail-proof itinerary?'

'Not now, Edie,' snapped Dylan, walking into the bathroom and slamming the door behind him.

And at first I wasn't too bothered. There was a difference to Dylan being ratty because he was sleep-deprived, and *us* not talking. But this morning he just pushed his Lumberjack Slam breakfast around his plate and gave monosyllabic replies to my bright enquiries about what he wanted to do today.

The only useful information I could get out of him was that he was bored with Chicago and he wanted to get on the road again.

'I suppose we should head in the direction of North Dakota,' I said as we started to drive out of Chicago. 'I'll just check what route we need to take.'

Dylan cleared his throat. 'We have to talk about that.'

I raised my eyebrows at him. 'Is that what got you out of bed in the middle of the night? Did I make a mistake on the itinerary?'

Dylan's hand shook slightly as he adjusted the rearview mirror. 'I don't want to go that way. I've changed my mind.'

'Er, why?' I asked, trying to keep my voice calm.

Dylan's face was set in grim lines. 'I want to head to Kentucky and then maybe Tennessee, we might have to go through Louisiana, Texas, Arizona and then LA.'

I stared at him. 'What?' I demanded incredulously.

'I don't want to go your way,' he insisted grimly.

'Pull over!' I demanded furiously but Dylan ignored me. I didn't know what he was thinking, which weirded me out almost as much as his sudden brain implosion. I can read Dylan pretty well but this . . . this was entirely out of my realm of experience. His whole body was tense, his knuckles white as they clutched the steering wheel.

I reached out and covered his hand with mine.

'Dylan, what is going on with you?' I said gently.

He knocked my hand away.

'I don't want to talk about it,' he said through gritted teeth.

'Oh God!' I half-screamed in frustration. 'Pull over. NOW!'

Dylan yanked the wheel, cutting through two lanes of traffic to the accompaniment of car horns and pulled in to the side of the road.

'You want to add weeks to our journey and you don't want me to ask why?' I started, but Dylan just crossed his arms and wouldn't look at me.

'I'm just asking you to do this one thing for me,' he snarled. 'I don't see what the big deal is.'

I waved the notebook with the itinerary in his face angrily and started ranting at him. Which probably wasn't the most beneficial way to handle Dylan's sudden freaky mood shift but it made me feel a lot better.

'You couldn't tell me before we left Washington which would have saved us a week in the car?' I berated him. 'Was it so difficult to say, "Edie, I think your schedule sucks and I've spent two years telling you I want to go to Seattle but I've changed my mind and would like to spend weeks driving through the Deep South during the hottest part of the year"? You are such a jerk sometimes.'

That got through to him, he snatched the notebook out of my hand and tossed it out of the window, catching my arm on his watch-strap in the process and ripping the skin.

I sucked the damaged flesh into my mouth. 'What the hell is wrong with you?'

Dylan turned on me, his eyes flashing furiously. 'If

you loved me Edie, you'd trust me and you'd shut up for one bloody minute!'

'Dylan,' I said deliberately, trying desperately to keep my temper. 'We're in this together, OK?'

'You don't have to talk to me like I'm mentally challenged,' he interrupted.

That did it. 'I prefer the term retarded,' I sniped. 'You just spring this on me and I have no comeback, because bottom line is you're driving.'

'That just about covers it,' agreed Dylan. 'Can we go now?'

He turned the key in the ignition and shot out into the road.

'You are bloody unbelievable—' I began but before I could finish my sentence about just what a dickhead he was, Dylan reached forward and switched the radio on so loud, it drowned out the sound of my voice.

'You can't just shut me out, D,' I sighed. 'And could you make some effort to keep to the speed limit?'

Baton Rouge – Memphis – Nashville

11th August

Things haven't got any better since then, which is, like, the understatement of all time. We drove into the Deep South a few days ago and have carried on driving all day and every day with the temperature a very uncool one hundred degrees in the shade. I feel like my insides are slowly drying up and it's all I can do to persuade Dylan to stop every hour so I can buy big bottles of water to replace all the fluids we're sweating out. I'm living in a halter top and some cut-off jeans that I wash out by hand every night while Dylan sits in front of a TV, glassy-eyed and not speaking.

I'm a lot worried that he's having some kind of breakdown. I know that his mum isn't exactly the poster-child for sanity but I thought that was due to Dylan's dad walking out on them. Now I'm beginning to wonder if maybe it is, like, hereditary. A couple of times I've contemplated phoning Shona but it seems wrong somehow. Like an intrusion or something.

What's even more worrying isn't the day-long

silences or the way Dylan's started ordering motel rooms with twin beds, like he can't stand the thought of touching me. It's that we get to another town (and by now we're not even going in a straight line but zigzagging across Kentucky and Nashville in a random pattern) and Dylan drops me in the city centre (or to be more precise practically pushes me out of the car) and tells me that he'll be back to pick me up in a couple of hours. Sometimes he'll be on time but once I waited five hours in the blistering heat and had to spend the next two days in bed suffering from heatstroke and watching the motes of dust dancing softly in the sunlight that streamed through the closed curtains while Dylan was God knows where.

I've tried talking to him about why he'd changed the route and whether I'd pissed him off but he either mutters that he doesn't want to talk about it or just refuses to say anything.

I used to feel like I'd known Dylan for a lifetime but I've spent the last nine days sitting next to him in that stupid car and he's become a tight-mouthed stranger. Someone I can't reach; someone I'm not even allowed to touch any more.

Jackson, Mississippi

13th August

Dylan went AWOL this morning. When I woke up all his stuff was gone. We'd left most of our gear in the boot of the car last night so he'd also taken most of my stuff with him.

I looked around the room, I went into the bathroom, I even walked over to the motel office to see if he was there but he'd vanished. I sat outside our room, not wanting to go back in because he wasn't there and if I walked back into that empty room I'd have to confront the fact that he wasn't *there*. I could feel a wave of panic hitting me, leaving me cold and clammy despite the heat. What was I meant to do? Was he coming back? Should I go to the police? Should I call my parents? No, scratch that. They'd probably get the next flight out to haul my sorry ass home. Oh God, I was even starting to think like an American.

In the end I mooched downtown, feeling particularly white trash in my flip-flops and pink straw hat.

I realised that cut-off denims and a retro Seventies vest (picked up in a Memphis thrift shop) that had 'Hangin' Loose' printed on it wasn't considered appropriate daywear to the God-fearing Baptist folk of Jackson from the disapproving glances I was getting. I caught a glimpse of myself in a shop window. I looked like some skeezy teen prostitute, no wonder Dylan had walked out (or driven out) on me. I wondered idly why his dad had walked out on his mum. He'd never talked about it. Maybe if I'd made more of an effort to find out about his family life I could understand why he'd been acting so oddly.

At least when I finally found a cool coffee shop with free wifi, the girl behind the counter looked like she wasn't still stuck in the Fifties. In fact, her platinum hair and black lace vest reminded me a lot of Poppy and I was hit with such a pang of homesickness that I nearly started crying.

She gave me a curious look as I very quietly ordered an iced tea and asked for the wifi password.

There were five emails from Grace wanting to know why I hadn't written for so long. I skipped through them. It was more of the same. Jack blah blah. Poppy blah blah. I don't know what to do blah blah. The last one read:

To: cutiesnowgirl@hotmail.com
From: graceofmyheart@hotmail.com

Where are you? Poppy says you and Dylan have probably eloped and gone to Vegas to get hitched. You haven't, have you?

We're on tour now. It's going well. That is, the being-on-stage bit is going well but Atsuko and Darby are snogging anything with a pulse, Poppy and Jesse are being all superior about everything and disappearing for long bouts of time (you were right, they are so having sex!!!!) which means that Jack and I are forced together all the time. I tried being aloof and mysterious like you suggested but Poppy told me off for acting like a stuck-up cow. Sometimes we talk about really deep things like if there are millions of different versions of us in different parallel universes doing all the things that we decided not to do. And other times we just play this game where you have to go through the alphabet naming things you'd take on a picnic. You know the one I mean?

Anyway, please, please write back.

Your rockin' pal

Grace xxx

I loved Grace but her problems just seemed so adolescent. Oh God, that sounded harsh. But they were high school problems and I was stuck in a weirdy, redneck town and my chronically depressed boyfriend was gone.

And everything she wrote about made me more and more tempted to get on the next plane home and penalty fees and non-transferable tickets be damned. The only person I wanted to talk to was Poppy.

I sent a quick reply back to Grace telling her that I was still alive, still unmarried but would write properly soon and then, with a quick wave to the girl behind the counter, I walked out on to the street and scrolled down my contacts till I found Poppy's number. My finger wavered over the 'call' button and holding my breath, I pressed.

It rang a couple of times and then I heard Poppy's voice.

'Edie?'

'Hi.'

'Where are you?'

'I'm in Mississippi.'

'Oh. So did you want to talk to Grace? This must be costing you a fortune.'

'No, I just called to say hi. To you. So, hi.'

'Are you OK? You sound upset. Is Dylan there?'

'No. I'm fine. Dylan's not here.'

'Are you sure you're all right?'

'I wish you were here. I miss you.'

'Yeah, well, whatever.'

'No, I mean, I really miss you. I'm . . . Dylan's . . .'

'Edie, what's the matter? Are you in trouble?'

'No, everything's good. I've got to go.'

'No, don't go. Do you want me to get your mum to call you?'

'No! I'm OK, I shouldn't have called. Dylan's coming, I have to go.'

The second I finished the call, I realised what a stupid mistake I'd made. I haven't spoken to Poppy properly in months and then I make a sudden freakish phone call which has either pissed her off even more or left her worried enough to think that calling my mother would be a good idea. But hearing her voice, while I stood in a street on the other side of the world, where none of the buildings or the people or even the shops were familiar, made me wish I was stuck in that smelly, cramped Transit van with Poppy, Atsuko and Darby. Because then I'd belong.

I bought a couple of bottles of water and some fruit and trailed aimlessly back to the motel to sit and wait and hope that Dylan would come back. I'd painted my toenails, given myself a facial, plucked my eyebrows, trimmed my fringe, watched lots of crappy TV and done some yoga exercises. Anything to fill the time. But the sky was deepening out to a dark blue and it was getting late and I had to face up to the fact that he might not be coming back.

I was rummaging in my bag for the travellers' cheques to see how much money I had left if I needed to get home when I found the print-out of the email Dylan had sent me in Chicago. All the worry and fear that had been buried deep inside me all day suddenly welled up and I was clutching the piece of paper to my chest and bawling my eyes out. It wasn't the kind of crying that I do when I've had a row with someone or when I'm watching *Lost In Translation* for the hundredth time and he touches her foot. My body was literally racked with sobs; I couldn't even stand up. I collapsed between the bed and the wall and cried like my heart was breaking. And that's what it felt like – that my heart was literally smashed to pieces.

At some stage I stumbled to the bathroom and stood in front of the mirror, as if I could will the crying to stop. My whole face was distorted with grief, my mouth this dripping, large, open *thing*, snot coming out of my nose and my eyes swollen and wet. I splashed my face with cold water and forced myself to take deep breaths. Crying was not going to help. I needed a plan. And I needed to sit down and confront all the thoughts that I hadn't wanted to think. Going to the police and reporting Dylan as missing was becoming a real possibility because I was scared that he was depressed enough to do something stupid.

I walked out of the bathroom, rubbing my face with a towel and still hiccuping gently when I realised Dylan was standing in the doorway. We looked at each other for a long second. I was so relieved to see him that for a moment I couldn't move.

But then I flew at him and slapped him hard round

the face. The sound of my hand connecting with his cheek reverberated round the room. Still Dylan just stood there with a blank expression on his face. I went berserk; hitting and punching his chest while I screamed at him.

'Have you any idea what I've been going through?' I yelled as he looked at me like he was seeing me for the first time. 'I thought you weren't coming back, I thought you'd had a crash. I've been out of my mind with worry.'

As I said that, my hands stopping whacking every spare inch of him that I could find and pulled him towards me and I hugged him tight enough for rib breakage if I hadn't been so puny.

One of his hands reached up to gently stroke my hair while the other traced small circles on my back.

'I'm sorry,' he whispered.

I pulled away from him slightly so I could look him in the eye. He winced slightly at the sight of my blotchy face.

'If you have a problem, you tell me about it,' I managed to get out between sobs. 'You don't do this ever again. And you look bloody awful.'

He smiled at that which just seemed to make the dark circles around his eyes and the smudges dusted over his cheekbones worse.

'I'm sorry,' he repeated, clutching me tighter and then I noticed a movement by the open door as a tall man who looked vaguely familiar stepped into the room.

'Are you ready?' he asked Dylan.

I looked at the man and then back at Dylan and just as the thought was forming in my head, Dylan turned to me and said, 'Edie, this is my dad.'

I almost went into cardiac arrest as Dylan put a name to the man hovering in the doorway. Dylan's *dad* was like a craggier, paunchier version of Dylan, his chocolate-brown hair streaked with grey. It was unnerving to see Dylan's green eyes staring out of someone else's face. I stood there shocked into speechlessness for the first time in my life until Dylan gently shook me. 'Eeds, get your stuff,' he said. 'We're going to stay with Lenny and Estella.'

'We're gonna what with who?' I managed to say, still looking from Dylan to his dad, who was watching me with a wary expression, and back to Dylan again.

Dylan quickly got my stuff together. I followed him into the bathroom where he was packing my shower bag and shut the door.

'What is going on?' I hissed quietly.

'I promise I'll tell you everything but later,' Dylan whispered back. 'Please, just bear with me a little bit longer.'

I shut my eyes for a second and felt the room spin around me. When I opened them again, I was still in the motel bathroom with Dylan's dad waiting for us outside.

'OK,' I finally agreed. 'But you have got some serious explaining to do.'

I didn't wait for Dylan to finish. I walked back into the other room, shoved my feet into my flip-flops and stalked out of the front door that Dylan's dad was holding open for me.

The E-zee Trailer Park, Jackson, Mississippi

13th August (later)

In the car, Lenny and Dylan made desultory conversation about local landmarks and how long we were going to stay. Dylan tried to talk to me a couple of times and I murmured responses but I was still in a state of shock. Which didn't improve when we got to the trailer and I was almost swept off my feet by a blonde, honey-skinned woman who pressed me to her unmistakably silicone chest.

'Oh, you must be Edie,' she drawled in one of those ridiculous Southern accents that you only hear on documentaries about child beauty pageants. 'You are just the cutest thing. Lenny, ain't she adorable?'

Lenny shifted uncomfortably and I realised I was being rude.

'Hello,' I said shyly. 'It's very nice to meet you.'

Can you say lame? But where's the etiquette book on how to handle these awkward social situations?

'I love your accent,' cooed Estella, wrapping an arm round me and leading me up the steps and into the trailer. 'So I guess you've had some surprises tonight. Dylan turning up with his long-lost daddy and . . .'

I stopped listening to what she was saying 'cause sitting on a hideous floral-patterned sofa were two pint-sized Dylans. Dylan's mini-mes.

'Mom, why is she staring at us?' said one of them.

I turned to Dylan who'd just come through the door. 'Anything else I should know about?' I asked him. 'You got grandparents in the trailer next door?'

'Now honey, I know you're upset,' interrupted Estella, resting a hand lightly on my arm. 'And I've told Dylan what a naughty boy he is to be so secretive, but we're glad to have you here, sweetheart. All of Lenny's family reunited.'

I was tempted to scream that they were no family of mine but, hey, good manners and all that, so I smiled tightly and patted Estella's hand.

'It's very nice to be here,' I said. None of this was her fault. 'You have a lovely hou— trailer. You've done very nice things with it.'

OK, it seemed to have electric lighting and satellite TV, but it was still a trailer.

Estella beamed at me. 'You and Dylan will have to sleep with the twins. They can have one bunk and you can have the other. Just as well you're both so skinny, huh?'

* * *

Dinner was difficult. Estella had cooked us roast beef even though it was ninety-five degrees outside. I tried to force it down but all I could do was look at Lenny and then Dylan and then the mini-mes who gave me the evil eye right back. It was so unreal that at one stage I got an attack of the giggles which I managed to hide as a choking fit while Estella fussed around getting me a glass of some toxic juice drink called Kool Aid and Dylan pinched my thigh under the table.

I couldn't talk to Lenny. Out of the four of them, he was freaking me out the most. Occasionally I could feel his eyes on me, but most of the time he was watching Dylan closely, as if he wanted to memorise every centimetre of him. It seemed that since leaving his job as a lecturer in Fine Art (at Dylan's university!) and abandoning his family, he'd been wandering ever since. Lenny had spent time in each of the places we'd visited in the last couple of weeks and in Nashville he'd hooked up with Estella, the mini-Ds putting in an appearance nine months later. The four of them didn't seem to have had a permanent address since. And as for gainful employment, Lenny had been a sign writer, guitarist in a country and western band, directed mud wrestling videos and was currently a wedding photographer which seemed kind of ironic as the man obviously had serious commitment issues.

After dinner, Dylan muttered something about going for a walk and after Estella gave us a torch and told us to look out for snakes (yes, snakes!), he grabbed my hand and hustled me outside.

We walked in silence for a few minutes until we came across a clear patch of grass and sat down. Dylan tried to reach for me but I pointedly ignored his outstretched hand.

'Start talking,' I ordered him flatly.

Most of it I'd already figured out. We'd been following the route that Lenny had taken, Dylan disappearing every day to check out his last known address and look for clues. Dylan had been thinking about finding Lenny as long ago as Washington and knew his dad had last been heard of in Chicago. He'd driven over to the trailer park this morning and sat all day with Estella waiting for Lenny to come home from some wedding in Utica . . .

When Dylan had finally finished the whole sorry tale, he lay back in the grass. The scent of magnolias was all around us, the crickets chirping along with the faint hum of traffic from the nearby interstate.

I sat with my knees pressed against my chest. 'Why didn't you tell me?' I said calmly. Although inside I was the complete opposite of calm.

'Because you'd have tried to talk me out of it,' Dylan answered immediately.

That hurt. 'You don't know that,' I argued. 'If you'd

explained to me that this is what you needed to do to be happy I would have understood.'

'Look, I couldn't deal with you and deal with all of this,' Dylan admitted. 'My dad was all I could think about. You don't know what it's like to have someone walk out on you.'

'I had a pretty good idea from about nine this morning,' I said sarcastically and Dylan wilted a bit.

'You don't get it,' he insisted. 'I had to find him. I had to have answers.'

'I understand,' I said fiercely.

'No, you don't!' Dylan sat up and squatted in front of me. 'Don't you see? I'm terrified that I'm going to turn out just like him. Never being able to settle in one place with one person. I had to find him to discover why he's done the things that he did.'

'That's just rubbish!' I said crossly. 'You're not your dad. OK, you might have some of his DNA, that doesn't mean you're a carbon copy of him. I mean, am I like my mother? And you'd better answer that really carefully.'

Dylan smirked. 'You aren't really like your mum but you do have certain scary facial expressions that you've inherited from her.'

I stuck my tongue out at him. 'And what about the twin rooms and the disappearing acts?'

Dylan rested his head in his hands. 'I handled things badly. I'm sorry for that. I just get so knee deep inside myself sometimes and not even you can pull me out. In fact, I don't want to be pulled out which I s'pose is why I pretended you weren't there.'

'All you tell me is that I have to trust you,' I said in a tiny voice. 'But when it comes to trusting *me* you just can't do it, can you? I could have been there for you. You didn't have to go through this alone.'

'I know that now and I'm sorry,' said Dylan, stroking my leg. He leant over and brushed his mouth against mine and I felt nothing.

'I don't know who you are any more,' I confessed. I placed one of my hands on his chest and felt his heart beating steadily. 'There's not enough room in there for me.'

I got to my feet and wrapped my arms around my body. Dylan wasn't Dylan any more, not *my* Dylan. He was part of them, those people back in the trailer. He belonged to Lenny and the mini-mes, and his mum, who I'd never met. And they probably had some handle on what made him tick 'cause I sure as hell didn't.

'Things are *not* all right with us,' I stated shakily. 'This stuff has happened and it can't unhappen. You don't love me . . .'

'I do!'

'You don't love me,' I continued as if Dylan hadn't spoken. 'Not in a good way. You weren't protecting me by not letting me in; you were shutting me out of your life. And I can't be . . . I don't want to be with someone who won't trust me.'

'So are you splitting up with me?' Dylan demanded in a choked voice. 'Are you going home?'

'I'm not going home. I'm going to stay with you because you need a friend,' I said. 'But that's all I'm going to be. No sex, no hands in places that they shouldn't be, no more giving you my heart so you can stamp all over it.'

And then I walked away, just left him kneeling in the long grass. Because if I'd stayed a moment longer he'd have seen the tears pouring down my face.

15th August

I spent most of this afternoon sitting on a creek bank, dangling my feet in the almost non-existent water and keeping an eye on Johnny and Hank, Dylan's four-year-old half brothers; sons of Lenny, Dylan's dad, and Estella, a twenty-five-year-old beautician from Tallahassee. Johnny and Hank, named after country singers Johnny Cash and Hank Williams. Note to self: Dylan is named after Bob Dylan. I can see a pattern emerging.

I stood up and walked over to Johnny and Hank. I can't tell them apart, while they can barely understand a word I say.

'What are you doing?' I asked.

'Looking for alligators,' said one of them. 'Then we're gonna poke 'em with sticks.'

There's not a lot you can say to that.

Oh God, I feel like I'm in a live recording of *The Jerry Springer Show*.

But I also feel quite content. After all that time on the road, it's good to stand still. Estella is sweet and ten times more in love with Lenny than he is with her. All she wants is for everyone to be happy. And if she can't make them happy, she'll settle for making them look nice. This is probably why she keeps offering to perm my hair because it's obvious to even Johnny and Hank that Dylan and I are not a happy couple. Or even an unhappy couple. We're two separate people again.

It doesn't help that Dylan and I have to sleep in a bed that measures two and a half feet across and is a blatant violation of my 'no inappropriate touching' rule. The first night, I scooted right over to the wall so there was a paper-thin gap between us. Things aren't any better during the day. Dylan spends most of the time with Lenny, who's about as talkative as his son. And I hang out with Estella who paints my nails and tells me that when she's a qualified beautician they're going to move to Hollywood.

'Edie? Why you got that funny look on your face?'

I snapped out of my daydream to find Johnny and Hank looking at me with identical 'that English girl is weird' expressions.

'I was just thinking about stuff,' I said. I never know how to talk to little kids, especially not these two.

When I'd asked them what they wanted to be when they grew up, Johnny said that he wanted to change his name to Fred and Hank had wanted to be a rabbit. Little freaks.

I was just showing them how to whistle using blades of grass when there was the sound of a twig breaking behind us. I turned round to see Lenny coming towards us. Johnny and Hank didn't seem to mind that their dad hardly ever spoke and started climbing all over him.

'Dinner's ready,' he said to me.

As we walked back to the trailer in silence, he told the boys to run ahead and touched my arm.

'What's going on with you and D?' he asked in a quiet voice.

That's *my* name for him, I thought, but I shrugged my shoulders. 'What's Dylan told you?'

'That you're mad at him for coming to find me,' said Lenny, looking me right in the eye. 'I don't like to see him hurt.'

I slowly exhaled and counted to ten. Lenny was a proper grown-up and it's hard to get angry with a proper grown-up, especially when it's someone's dad but he was pushing all my buttons, all at once.

'I'm not the one who hurt him,' I snapped. 'Dylan and I are none of your business. In fact Dylan is none of *your* business so don't start acting like you suddenly care.'

Lenny arched his eyebrow and looked so much like

Dylan that it was like someone twisting a knife in my gut. 'I haven't been around but that doesn't mean I stopped loving him,' he said.

'Well, I haven't stopped loving him either,' I said. 'But I do not want to be in a relationship with someone who . . . I don't want to talk about this with you.'

I crossed my arms and glared at Lenny, who smiled slightly. That just made me even more mad.

'I know you think I'm some stupid kid but I'm telling you if you hurt him again, you'll have to deal with me,' I warned him.

It was a stupid, over-dramatic thing to say but instead of laughing at me, Lenny nodded his head and said seriously, 'He's lucky to have someone like you as a friend.'

At ten, all the cicadas stop their creaking noise at once; almost as if someone's flicked a switch.

Estella lit citronella candles to keep away the mosquitoes and made us these minty, rum-soaked drinks called mojitos. It was very tense. Dylan and Lenny sat there with matching brooding expressions while Estella and I made polite conversation about the differences between America and Britain until I couldn't bear it any more and went to bed. There's only so much you can say about the differences between *EastEnders* and *The Young and the Restless*.

* * *

I couldn't sleep. I looked at the clock; it was 2am.

The sound of voices drifted in from outside. I tried not to listen. But the more I concentrated on not listening, the clearer the voices got.

'Your mother and me . . . we never got along . . . I was a lousy father . . . I was angry and resentful all the time.'

'I remember.' Dylan sounded cool.

'I thought about you all the time but you were better off without me. I left you a ton of money didn't I?'

'You mean *you* were better off without *me*. You never sent birthday cards or Christmas cards.'

'I thought I was doing the right thing.'

There was silence. I kicked off the tangled sheet and idly raised one of my legs, watched a trickle of sweat run down my calf.

'So you and the little girl?'

'Her name's Edie.'

'She's very young.'

'Why does everyone keep saying that? She's nineteen, I'm only twenty-one in case you've forgotten.'

'By the time I was your age I was a father.'

'Well, I'm not going to be making your mistakes.'

'But Edie, she's not like your mother . . . she's very strong.'

'You have no right to say that. You walked out on Mum after making her life a misery. You think I don't know about your girlfriends? You think I don't remember the way you'd stink of booze when you were driving me to school? You made her like she is.'

'You're right. But if I'd stayed then . . .'

'Well, we'll never know, will we?'

'I'm just saying that the little girl in there she's feisty as hell. You need a strong woman like that.'

'. . . Edie's not that strong. She's all over the place most of the time. She's changing every day. When I'm with her I feel like . . .'

I held my breath. It was like when you dream that you're falling and your heart misses a beat. I felt like I was pitching downwards with nothing to grab on to to steady my fall.

'Like what?'

'I don't want to talk about her with you. You don't know her. It's like, like she's changing so fast, trying to run in all these different directions and all I can do is follow her and hope that when she's ready to stop, I'll have caught up.'

'You don't have to catch up with her. You can do anything you want Dylan, you could come over here; go to a really good art school.'

'You're not listening to me. I don't want to be like you, constantly searching for some big dream that doesn't exist and making everyone around me unhappy. So what if I'm stuck in Manchester, so what if Edie's moving on . . .'

'You kids think first love is forever. It's not, Dylan. If she's moved on, then maybe you should too.'

'Screw you,' Dylan snarled. There was the sound of a chair being scraped back. 'You don't understand. People aren't just *things* that happen to you and then disappear, Edie and I were proper. She made me a better person and now I've lost her. And I don't want to move on. I want to stay where I am, with her.'

I sat up in bed and pushed the sweaty strands of my hair away from my face. Everything was so messed. I didn't want to split up with Dylan but once someone's done the things that he had, you can't undo those things. And just because I was the one who'd called it quits, didn't mean that I'd got away free from all the pain and misery that happens when you tell the love of your life that you don't want him to be the love of your life any more. The raw hurt in Dylan's voice echoed around the empty place in my chest where my heart used to be.

I lay back down and kicked the sheet off, hoping that some stray breeze would blow in through the window and cool me down. Instead, Dylan crept through the door. I'm such a coward that I pretended to be asleep. But Dylan crawled into bed and reached out to touch me. Still feigning sleep, I inched away because if he touched me I'd get all undone.

Then Dylan started crying. Quiet choked sobs and when I turned over and asked if he was all right, he practically threw himself into my arms. I rested his head on my chest and I stroked his hair and murmured soothing words that didn't really make any sense.

We didn't talk about it the next day.

Mississippi – Tennessee

16th August

Am I glad to be on the road again. Dylan's calmer after his crying thing. I s'pose he was so twisted up inside that he had to let it out. We're talking again. Which is good but being Edie the best friend, instead of Edie the girlfriend is not so good.

I mean, it was my decision, yeah? So I have to be all bright-faced and optimistic to show that it was the right decision. But I don't feel bright-faced and optimistic. Not at all.

But I'm also glad to get out of the trailer park, or the trailer to be more specific. Watching Estella and Lenny was not my favourite spectator sport. I couldn't stand the way she'd constantly ask his opinion about everything and how she'd start most sentences with, 'Lenny thinks' or 'Lenny says'. It wasn't her sappiness that got on my nerves; it was the way she was so hopelessly in love with someone who didn't love her back. I don't think Lenny loves anyone. Not even himself. He's what my nan would call a troubled soul.

Which probably explains why yesterday morning when we were leaving he was nowhere to be found. I hugged Estella and promised to keep in touch and even managed to ruffle the mini-Dylans' hair without flinching (nits were a big possibility). Then it was Dylan's turn to be pressed against Estella's amazing double E-cup mammaries and play-wrestle with Johnny and Hank. After that came the awkward hanging around while we waited for Lenny, and Estella tried to make excuses for him.

'D, we should get going,' I said eventually. 'He probably doesn't like goodbyes.'

'No change there then,' Dylan muttered darkly, as he got into the car.

I took the peanut butter and jelly (that would be jam) sandwiches that Estella had made for us and gave her one last hug.

'You take care honey,' she sniffed, giving me a little push towards the car. 'And you don't be a stranger, Dylan. I know your daddy's real proud of you but he don't like to get all emotional and . . .'

'Just drive,' I hissed at Dylan as I shut the car door. 'Or we'll be here forever.'

Estella was still apologising for Lenny as we drove off. I waved and waved until we cleared the trailer park entrance and I couldn't see her any more.

I glanced at Dylan. 'You OK, D?' I asked lightly.

'Yeah, I shouldn't have expected anything else from him,' he replied.

'Like Estella said, I just don't think he's good at showing his feelings,' I said carefully. 'Look, we've got miles to go so I'm going to take over the music selection and you just put your foot on the accelerator and worry about the driving.'

Dylan smiled a little. 'Thanks, Edie.'

'For what, bossing you about?' I laughed.

'You know what for,' murmured Dylan.

I was just turning the volume up on *Write about Love* and telling Dylan that he'd listen to Belle and Sebastian and damn well like it, when we saw Lenny standing at the side of the road.

I wanted to tell Dylan to carry on driving but he was already pulling over. Lenny opened one of the back doors and threw a bag inside. My internal Civil Defence System started clanging but Dylan was already jumping out of the car.

'What are you doing?' he asked Lenny who was in the process of joining his bag on the back seat.

'What does it look like?' said Lenny. 'I want out of this town. I need to be on the move again.'

I decided to stay where I was but I turned off Belle and Sebastian and studied one of the guidebooks very intently. Dylan had to handle this one on his own.

He started by grabbing the bag and handing it back to Lenny.

'You can't come with us,' he told him sternly. 'You've got a family to take care of.'

I tilted the windscreen mirror so I could see what was going on. Lenny had his hand on Dylan's shoulder.

'You don't understand. I feel like I'm trapped,' he tried to explain. 'I need to be free.'

Dylan shook his hand off. 'No, what you need is to show some responsibility for the first time in your life.'

'Dylan . . .'

'No, don't try and talk your way around it,' Dylan snapped wearily. 'You can't bail out every time things get difficult. Estella thinks the world of you, though I don't know why, and you have two sons who need a father.'

Lenny's shoulders slumped; he looked defeated. 'I thought it would be fun. A bonding thing.'

Dylan looked unimpressed. 'It's too late for us but it's not too late for you to go back to that bloody trailer and start acting like a grown-up.'

Way to go, D.

Dylan got back in the car and Lenny leant in at the open window. 'Don't hate me too much, Dylan,' he said with a wry smile. 'And don't forget about me.'

Dylan clasped Lenny's hand in an awkward grip. 'There's no danger of me forgetting you, Lenny,' he said wearily. 'We have to go, if Edie doesn't eat some fresh fruit and veg soon she'll get scurvy.'

I waved half-heartedly at Lenny. 'Well, bye then. Take care,' I said comfortingly. Be nice to Estella, I added to myself.

Lenny smiled at me. 'I hope you two work it out.' He banged on the roof of the car. 'Go on, get out of here.'

For the second time, we drove off.

I squirmed round on the seat so I could share a horrified glance with Dylan.

'Did that really happen?' I exclaimed in a bewildered voice.

'Oh yeah,' said Dylan.

'Are you upset?'

Dylan considered the question for a moment and then pulled a surprised face. 'Actually, no. I feel really relieved that we're out of there and I feel really good. Like, I've got rid of some of my demons.'

'Some of them?' I asked in a mock-scared voice. 'You mean there are *more*?'

'You're a real comedian, Eeds,' said Dylan sarcastically. 'A lot's happened, most of it my fault but I know the rest of the trip is going to be pain-free.'

'Why did you go and say that?' I snapped. 'You've jinxed us.'

'What*ever*, Miss Glass Half Empty!'

Bossier City, Louisiana

22nd August

To: cutiesnowgirl@hotmail.com
From: graceofyourheart@hotmail.com

Edie where are you? We're all freaked out and worried about you. Especially Poppy.
Please, please get in touch.
Lots of love Grace xxxx
PS: Your phone ain't working!

To: graceofmyheart@hotmail.com
From: cutiesnowgirl@hotmail.com

Hi Grace

It's Edie. The lesser-spotted Edie, that is. I am so sorry about disappearing on you. A long, long story. Stuff got really intense over here, hence stricken phone call to Poppy. There's no good way to say this so I'm just going to come right out with it: Me and Dylan have split up. Lots of reasons but mainly we're not the same people that we were when we first started going out with each other. But it's not all bad. We're really good mates and maybe we just mistook close friendship for something else. I've laughed so much in the last six days and we're more relaxed with each other than we have been in ages. The days before that were distinctly lacking in laughage, let me tell you.

We were in Mississippi, but the schedule's so out of whack that we tailed back to Memphis so we could go to Gracelands. It looks nothing like your bedroom! We bought loads of really tacky Elvis merchandise and our Elvis karaoke CD is the current in-car entertainment favourite.

Now we're cruising through Louisiana and should be in Texas tonight. We had to give New Orleans a miss but the guidebook says that it's the mugging capital of the States and Dylan reckons that we've managed to get this far without being involved in a drive-by shooting and it would be stupid to tilt the odds now.

I hope you are well and having a rockin' good time on tour. How's things with Jack? Have you snogged him yet?

Love you tons. And tell Poppy I'm sorry about phoning her. And that I love her tons too.

Edie xxx

PS: I'm writing this from a place called Bossier City. That's a funny place-name isn't it? Or have I been stuck in a car for too long?

Austin, Texas

24th August

Texas is big. The largest state in the union to be specific and men wear cowboy boots and stetsons with their business suits and not a hint of irony. And everyone says 'y'all'. As in 'Y'all have a nice day.'

Dylan and I have been having nice days. Lots of them. Now that the itinerary is gone, we meander from one place to another, enjoying the getting there as much as the being-there-and-getting-to-have-a-shower. But I was kidding myself if I thought we could be friends. We're not friends. We're two people who have split up and are trying to put a brave face on it.

'Cause even after all the crap that Dylan's put me through, I love him. And although rationally I realise that you can't be with someone who shuts you out all the time, I miss all the little things. Like Dylan driving with his hand resting on my knee and the way that we'd share a big, gooey ice cream but I especially miss the hot nights in those motel rooms when Dylan was all around me, the smell and taste and feel of him.

And I'd go to sleep in his arms with the sound of his heartbeat being the last thing I'd hear before I fell asleep. I ache with longing.

We sit opposite each other in diners and the brush of his leg against mine under the table makes me lose my appetite. And at night when we're lying in our twin beds and I hear Dylan's slow, even breathing and steal a glance at the smooth lines of his back and shoulders, I itch to creep across the room and touch him. What's even worse is when Dylan leans against me to change a CD. Or when the heat gets too much and he decides to pull off his T-shirt and drive bare-chested *and* he asks me to put sun cream on his back.

We don't talk about us though. We talk about everything but us. And when I hear Dylan talking about his art and how the trip has inspired him or even hear him spend half an hour musing on what kind of food he wants for dinner that night, it makes me love him even more. No, Edie! These are bad, bad thoughts.

El Paso, Texas

25th August

Dylan decided to teach me how to drive. Let me recount the many ways in which this was a stupid idea: I have very low concentration levels, even less co-ordination skills and I can't talk and do something else at the same time.

'I'm worn out from all the driving,' Dylan whined when we were still 200 miles from El Paso, Texas where we were meant to be spending the night. 'You have a go.'

'No,' I gasped. 'I don't know how to. I've never had a lesson in my life.'

Dylan looked unconcerned. 'It's easy. It's a straight road so you don't have to worry about steering, you put one foot on the accelerator pedal and when you want to stop, you press down on the brake pedal instead.'

'But what about the gear shift?' I asked in a terrified voice. 'No, I didn't say that. I'm not driving. We could get pulled over by the police. We'd get deported. My mum would kill me!'

Dylan stopped the car. 'It's OK. It's automatic – you just stick it in "drive" and then you don't have to do anything else. Come on, we haven't seen another car for miles. There isn't another town for miles so we have to get to El Paso and I have killer backache.'

'I could rub it for you,' I offered weakly. If I don't have to touch you while I'm doing it.

'Oh come on Eeds, don't be a chicken.'

I glared at him. 'I'm not being a chicken,' I protested. 'I'm being serious.'

'Bock, bock, bock,' said Dylan softly.

'Fine,' I snapped, unbuckling my seatbelt. 'But if we wind up dead then don't blame me!'

Driving was horrible with added bits of horribleness. There were loads of things to remember and it was boring.

Dylan made lots of encouraging noises but all I could concentrate on was the vast grey expanse of road in front of me. Dylan meanwhile propped his feet on the dash and leaned back in the seat luxuriously before putting on the Hank Williams CD he'd bought to remind him of the demon spawn that was his half brother.

'Turn it off,' I demanded. 'Put on something I know really well, otherwise I can't concentrate. New sounds, driving; too much to take in. And don't keep talking to me.'

'You were the one who was talking to me,' Dylan protested.

'I said don't talk to me!'

After 100 miles, Dylan took pity on me and we swapped over again. Secretly I was quite proud of myself. Driving was so grown up. But all that tense concentration had left me with a raging headache. I massaged my neck and closed my eyes.

The next thing I knew we were in El Paso and Dylan was driving into the car park of a Best Western Motel.

I slowly opened the car door and slid out, almost falling over. Dylan was at my side in a flash.

'You all right?' he asked in a concerned voice.

'Tired and headachey,' I mumbled. 'Let's check in and find somewhere to eat so I can go to bed.'

I lay on the bed and wondered why all motels came with a regulation brown floral quilt while Dylan brought our suitcases in. I felt very odd, almost as if I was floating.

The bed dipped as Dylan sat down. 'Edie? I just asked you three times if you were all right,' he said, pressing a hand to my forehead. 'You're very hot.'

I sat up and tried to ignore the rush of dizziness that almost sent me sprawling back on the bed.

'I'm hot because it is hot,' I grumbled. 'Can we just go and have dinner?'

Ignoring Dylan's outstretched hand, I got to my feet rather shakily and walked to the bathroom to splash my face with cold water.

He's having a shower now and I wish he'd hurry the hell up. I feel really icky . . .

27th August

To: shonawilliams@hotmail.com
From: artboy@hotmail.com

Hi Shona

It's Dylan here. I know we said we wouldn't get into the whole email thing but I really needed to talk to you. Even though you're not here. So I guess I'm going to put it all down in this email because that way you won't interrupt and I can make some sense of what's been happening over the last few weeks.

First thing that's causing me so much angst? Edie collapsed the other night and is in hospital. They don't know what's wrong with her. I feel so guilty. I made her drive the car because I was tired and even though she really didn't want to do it she showed willing. When we got to El Paso (that's in Texas, I know you're crap at Geography), she was acting weird. Disorientated and complaining of a headache. We went out to get something to eat in this Mexican place. I should have known something was wrong right then because she hates Mexican food. Well, she pushes the food round her plate and can't quite hold a conversation, her replies are distant and not exactly in the right places. But when I ask her what the matter is, she gets all mad.

So we're sitting there when she suddenly says she doesn't feel well and wants to go to bed. So we walk across the road to our motel and I'm practically holding her up by this stage. Which is another sign that something was seriously wrong because we have this whole 'no wrong touching' rule (but oh, you don't know about that – I'll tell you about that later). We get to the motel room and she falls on to the bed so I decide that she'll be all right after some sleep. I'm just cleaning my teeth when Edie suddenly lurches into the bathroom, doesn't even make it to the loo, throws up all over the floor and then suddenly falls to her knees and slumps forwards. When I get to her and pull her up, I realise that she can't even see me. Just before she lost consciousness, her eyes were trying to focus on me but rolling right up so all I could see were the whites.

She's in hospital now (thank God we have medical insurance sorted out). She's not in a coma or anything but she's not making a whole lot of sense. Keeps drifting in and out of sleep and is pretty much incoherent most of the time. The doctors are doing tests, they've taken vials and vials of blood but no-one seems to know what's actually wrong with her. At one stage they thought it might be meningitis and, in one of Edie's rare moments of awakeness, gave her a spinal tap, which was just horrible. She cried all the way through it because it hurt so much. Now they're talking about allergies and viral infections.

She looks very small and frail. The hospital gown's too big for her and she's got a drip in her arm. I don't know what to do, Shona. When she passed out, her breathing was so faint that I thought she was going to die.

I had to phone her mum who wanted to get on the first flight available but her dad talked to me and realised that there wasn't much they could do. I promised that I'd look after Edie before we went and all I've done is cause her physical and mental anguish.

Mental anguish? I can just picture you giving me one of your disapproving looks. Because before all this happened, I acted like a grade one arse. I had this stupid idea that I was going to find my dad. I think it was in the back of my mind even when we first started talking about going to the States. I mean, I knew that he'd been in Chicago. But instead of telling Edie, I just embarked on this wild goose chase around most of the Southern states. And I got all scary and closed off. I even scared myself. I wouldn't tell Edie what was going on. In fact, I more or less stopped talking altogether. All I could think about was finding him and I couldn't let anything get in the way, not even Edie. I just kept telling her to trust me. Because I really thought I could do this and *then* clear it all up with Edie.

I was awful, Sho! I'd just dump Edie in these

strange towns and tell her I'd pick her up in a couple of hours and then go to look for my dad. The day that I did find him, I left while she was still sleeping and didn't get back till it was almost dark. I've never seen Eeds so angry, she started beating me up and then held me so tight I thought my ribs were going to break.

That night she broke up with me. I'd said that I was sorry and tried to explain but she started banging on about how I didn't trust her and I didn't love her in the right way. It would have been better if she'd flown home but she decided that we'd be friends and she was going to stick around. But I don't think she ever loved me. You can't go from being lovers to friends as easily as she has if you really loved someone.

At first I thought she'd come round, get over it once the dust had settled, but she was serious. While we were staying with my dad (I'm getting to that bit) we had to sleep together in a single bed and I'd spend most of the night gritting my teeth and trying not to think about touching her. I'd find ways to touch her anyway, little sly brushes of her leg when I'm driving, I'd ask her to put sun cream on me and half hope that she'd be so overcome with lust that she'd pounce on me but the girl's mind is made up.

So my dad? Laughing Lenny. I'm glad that I found him but only because it made me realise that I was better off without him. He's involved with this really mad woman called Estella, huge plastic boobs and huge blonde hair, not the brightest bulb in the box. And

I have twin half brothers called (and you'll love this) Hank and Johnny. Edie thought they were devil's spawn and kept telling me that they probably had 666 marked on their heads. Lenny hasn't changed, still a self-obsessed loser. Can't settle in one place or in one job or with one woman. He told me he had another girlfriend in the next town and he wanted to come with me and Edie when we left. I told him to go back and make things all right with him and Estella but I get the feeling he won't be there for much longer. I was always worried that I was going to turn out just like him but I don't think that any more. It's like *I'm* in charge of what happens to me, not him. But having said that, I wouldn't have lost Edie if I'd been more honest and open with her. How can she think I don't love her when she's the only person who means more to me than I do? What meeting Lenny really proved is that family isn't the people who you're related to by blood and all that, it's the people that you choose to love. And Edie's my family.

So that's the whole sad story. I could tell you about all the places we've been but, hey, read a guidebook. I'm going back to the hospital now and I guess I'll see you when (if?) we ever get home. You're going to see Mellowstar's last gig in London, right?

Sorry for over-sharing

Dylan x

To: artboy@hotmail.com
From: shonawilliams@hotmail.com

Dylan

You are such an arse! No wonder Edie broke up with you. If she was me, you'd be getting used to life without your kneecaps.

I'm seriously freaking out about our girl. I hope Edie will pull through – it sounds like she's been so stressed out that it's no wonder she's ill. But she's a tough little critter and I *know* she'll be making your life hell in a couple of days' time. Just because she can.

I'm going to give you some advice although you don't deserve it. I think she does still love you. And I think if she didn't care about you in such a big, important way she would have come home. I'm not convinced about this whole friend thing. I don't think you and Edie will ever be friends, you'll either be in love or you'll hate each other. If you want to get her back, you have to show her that you love her. And you have to do some serious grovelling. I'd start with jewellery and work your way up!

As for your dad, I'm really, really glad that you went looking for him. I don't exactly approve of your methods but I think you really needed to get 'some closure' (assume cheesy American accent here).

Let me know what's happening with you, you big jerk.
Love
Sho
(No kisses for you 'cause you ain't worthy of them.)

El Paso Memorial Hospital, Texas

28th August

When I woke up this morning I was in a hospital bed, with a drip in my arm and Dylan asleep in a chair next to me. Oh and my insides felt like someone had rubbed sandpaper along them.

I leant over, which hurt a lot, and prodded Dylan who came to with a start.

'D, what's going on?' My voice sounded rusty. 'I remember throwing up yesterday.'

Dylan clutched my hands. 'Edie, you've been in hospital for three days!'

I frowned which also hurt a lot. 'Oh yeah, I remember someone doing something painful to my back.'

Dylan was pressing a buzzer. 'They were giving you a spinal tap, they were taking fluid from your spine, it was awful. You cried all the way through it,' he said with a grimace. 'How do you feel?'

'Crappy,' I replied. 'My throat really hurts.'

'You had an endoscopy.'

'I had a whatty?' I asked, sitting forward. 'Can you straighten these pillows for me?'

Dylan rushed forward and started plumping up my pillows and fussing with the bedclothes. 'They stuck a tube with a camera down your throat 'cause they thought you might have an internal bleed somewhere.'

I pulled a face. 'Ewwww!'

Just then a nurse came into the room. Check, I was in a private room.

'Oh you're back with us,' she said brightly. 'I'm Cathy. How do you feel?'

I opened my mouth to answer her and she shoved a thermometer in before wrapping a cuff round my upper arm and pumping a rubber bulb attached to it until she almost cut off my circulation.

'I'm just checking your blood pressure,' she said when I made ouch faces.

'What's wrong with me?' I asked, when she took the thermometer out of my mouth.

'I'll get Dr Greenbaum to come in and see you,' Cathy replied. 'But your temperature's down a couple of degrees and your blood pressure's almost normal.'

'Can I have some water?'

Dylan was already on his feet. Cathy smiled at him. 'Dylan why don't you come with me and we'll get Edith some ice?'

I settled back down. 'D?'

He turned round and looked at me expectantly. 'I'm hungry,' I whined. 'Can I have some ice cream?'

Dylan looked at Cathy. 'I think she's feeling better. Can I get her some ice cream?'

'After she's been checked over,' Cathy said firmly, holding the door open for Dylan.

Dr Greenbaum was there within minutes and after poking and prodding and saying 'uh-uh' a lot as he asked me loads of questions, he said I was over the worst of it.

'Over the worst of what?' I asked.

'Oh, probably a non-specific viral infection,' he replied breezily. 'You're young, you're in good health; you should rally round in no time. You gave us quite a fright.'

'So when can I leave?'

I saw Dylan peering through the glass panel in the door and I beckoned for him to come in.

Dr Greenbaum carried on. 'We want to keep you in for another twenty-four hours and then you need to take it easy for a little while.'

'So we can carry on driving to LA?'

'No we can't,' interrupted Dylan. 'We are booking into a hotel and then we're flying back home.'

'We have to go to LA,' I argued. 'I'll be sitting in a car. Selecting our song stylings and giving you directions is not exactly strenuous.'

Dylan had a mutinous expression on his face but Dr Greenbaum smiled. You could tell he was thinking, hey what a crazy pair of kids.

'OK, time out, guys,' he said. 'A hotel would be a good idea for three or four days and then you can get back on the road.'

'I told you,' I said smugly to Dylan.

'But regular rest breaks,' continued Dr Greenbaum. 'And if you're going to the Grand Canyon, no hiking. Take the helicopter tour instead.'

'So, can I have some ice cream now?' I asked.

Dr Greenbaum nodded and Dylan rolled his eyes. 'At least when you were ill, you weren't so demanding. What flavour?'

The Holiday Inn, El Paso, Texas

30th August

Staying in a hotel is so much more fun than motel living. I was angsting about the cost but Dylan insisted that we had plenty of money left and during the difficult phone call home when I had to persuade my parents that I wasn't dying any more, they were adamant that we should use the credit card to pay for a hotel.

In fact, my mother was contemplating chartering a plane to fly me home but Dad took the phone off her, asked me a few pertinent questions about my general well-being and told me to ignore her.

Dylan has been annoyingly kind. I guess having your girlfriend, I mean ex-girlfriend, throw up and then pass out on you is a bit of a shock. He's bought me flowers, more ice cream than I know what to do with and even sourced some Ribena. Every time I stand up, he hovers next to me and generally treats me like the princess that he used to accuse me of being.

I insisted that we went out for dinner tonight

because much as I love staying in a hotel I was going stir crazy.

'Are you sure you're ready?' he kept asking as I put make-up on for the first time in weeks.

'I'm fine,' I told him for the fiftieth time. 'This is a dry run and then we're getting in the car tomorrow and heading for Arizona.'

Dylan refused to commit. 'We'll see,' he said.

The other benefit to being ill is the fact that I've lost so much weight that I feel it's my duty to eat as much as possible. I'm talking three meals a day plus hourly snacks.

'I must be iron deficient,' I told Dylan as I started cutting into a steak that was the size of my plate. The chips came in a separate bowl.

Dylan looked slightly horrified as he picked at his chicken Caesar salad. 'It's too hot to eat,' he pointed out.

I shrugged. 'I've missed out on four days of eating. And I've lost a stone. That's fourteen pounds! Surely it's not possible to lose that much weight in such a short amount of time. They don't tell you that at Weight Watchers!'

'I don't know how you can joke about it,' he said, pinching a handful of my chips.

'Well I feel fine now,' I stated, smacking his hand. 'It was probably worse for you than for me. I mean, I didn't know what was going on.'

Dylan put down his fork. 'I thought you were going to die,' he said quietly. 'And I went to pieces. There were two paramedics checking your airway and asking me how long you'd been unconscious and I couldn't even speak. I didn't even think about starting resuscitation until they got there.'

Dylan looked so racked with guilt that I didn't know what to do.

'Well, I *had* just been sick,' I teased. '*I* wouldn't have wanted to get too close to me.'

'Don't joke about it!' Dylan exclaimed. 'I don't know what I'd have done if you'd died.'

I touched his hand across the table and he wound his fingers through mine and didn't let go. Dylan looked deep into my eyes like he was trying to tell me something deep and profound. Then with one last squeeze he let go of my hand.

'Maudlin much!' I said lightly, to try and defuse some of the tension. 'I'm not going to waste another minute worrying about "what ifs" and "might have beens". I feel loads better and that's all that matters.'

It seemed like Dylan was going to argue the point but he thought better of it. 'I guess you're right,' he muttered. But he shot me another loaded look as if to suggest that me feeling loads better wasn't all that mattered. Not even close.

Albuquerque, New Mexico

2nd September

I can't stop thinking about Dylan's mouth . . .

Did I really write that? No matter how I try to condition myself to keep my Dylan emotions on the friendship setting, these strange treacherous thoughts creep in. When he's concentrating on something, the tip of his tongue creeps out of the corner of his mouth and I'm mesmerised by it.

And when I crack a funny and Dylan does his usual I-don't-want-to-encourage-her-but-I-have-no-control-over-my-mouth smirk, I remember how he used to kiss me and I could *feel* him smiling.

Like I said, I can't stop thinking about Dylan's mouth.

Dylan is still being an über sweetie. It's actually becoming quite a strain. I wish he'd crack under the pressure and revert to his usual sardonic self. Fr'instance we're meant to be back on a schedule, we have seven days to get to LA and drop off the car but he made a day's detour because I said in passing that it might have been interesting if we could go to Roswell and check out the UFO museum.

And if I so much as stretch my arms because I'm getting stiff from sitting for so long, he insists on stopping the car and making me lie down on the back seat so 'You can have a nap'. To be quite frank, he's treating me like a frail, elderly auntie. But Roswell was, well, kind of cool. No alien sightings though.

Flagstaff, Arizona

3rd September

To: cutiesnowgirl@hotmail.com
From: graceofmyheart@hotmail.com

Oh Edie

I'll quickly ask after your health and hope you haven't done any projectile vomiting lately. But that was only to be polite and now we need to talk about me!

So when you last heard from me things were all right with Jack. No great progress and no smooching but I really felt like we had a connection and maybe I was laying the groundwork to smooching. But now he's shown himself to be just like other boys! He's turned into a player. And obviously I blame Jesse. Everything is always Jesse's fault. It was Jesse who decided that being cooped up in a van with four girls all day meant that him and Jack were 'getting too in touch with their feminine sides'. So Jesse has started referring to us as 'his bitches' which Poppy, Atsuko and

Darby think is hysterically funny and Jack has started hitting on girls!

Apparently knowing how to hook up a PA system turns boys into complete gods. I can't see it myself. All these girls come up to him after we've played and last night he got off with this horrible skank who was at least in her early twenties. I used to be the only person who saw something special in Jack and now it's like all these girls are after him as they think he's cool because he hangs out with a band. A band that I'm in! They don't see the special side of him, the side that I see. But that doesn't stop him from snogging them and telling me to go away when I say that I have to speak to him! I was only going to ask if he wanted a drink but he was all like, 'Not now Gracie, I'm busy,' and then him and the skanky ho started laughing at me! I hate him. And I'm never going to find anyone who wants to kiss me. Or sees something special in me.

The only good thing is that in ten days, I'll see you again! I really, really can't wait. And yesterday when Jesse was being too much even for Poppy to handle she gave a deep sigh and said, and I quote, 'It's at times like this that I wish Edie was here so she could give you a lecture about the finer points of third-wave feminism.' I know Poppy's all psyched about seeing you and keeps asking me if you've dropped any hints about presents that you might have bought for her!

Anyway, Jesse's standing in front of the window of Caffè Nero and pulling faces at me, which is his

Neanderthal way of saying that I have to get back in
the van.
Love you
Gracie xxxxx

I really felt for Grace. I could relate to her pain and
the pain was not a friend. Dylan was sitting next to me
and looking through the maps for about the millionth
time to see how quickly we could get to Los Angeles via
Las Vegas. I'd told him till I couldn't tell him any more
that it was a bloody five hour drive. Five hours! Pfffft!
That's nothing compared to how far we've already
come. But he was starting to get really antsy about
having the car back in time. Not to mention repeatedly
telling me this without raising his voice or being
sarcastic. I never thought I'd miss Dylan being a sarky
git but, oh, I so do.

To: graceofmyheart@hotmail.com
From: cutiesnowgirl@hotmail.com

Hey sweet thing

I am in the rudest health. No projectile vomiting or
headaches but thanks for asking. Jack is displaying
all the symptoms of boy disease. And he's acting like
an idiot for no other reason than because he can. I
also think that he's trying to make you jealous but I'd
have to do some in-the-field research to be sure of

that. It's like boys have penises and they think their penises are so great that they can act like complete prats ninety-nine per cent of the time and still be cool. All because of their penises. Well, that's my theory anyway.

Dylan doesn't act like a prat though. Very rarely. He doesn't act all 'hey little girl, I'm the boss because I have a penis' with me. Well, hardly ever. I love him to bits. But as a friend. Strictly as a friend. Don't start thinking that we've got back together because we so haven't. We made a rational decision to break up and we're both grown-ups and handling it very sensibly. And it's easy to think of him as my friend and nothing else. Oh, the friend thing is working out fine. It's all kinds of fine. Yeah . . .

Anyway, this is the travelogue bit; so pay attention. I'm in a small college town called Flagstaff in Arizona and we've just driven through this place called The Petrified Forest which is full of, wait for it, petrified trees. It's something to do with fossils and silica and I'll shut up 'cause I don't know what I'm going on about. We're heading towards the Grand Canyon. It's seriously too hot to hike through it (does the temperature ever drop below one hundred degrees in this country?) and although my lovely Dr Greenbaum at El Paso Memorial Hospital said we should take a helicopter ride, Dylan and I are too chicken. We've already started mentally preparing ourselves for the plane ride home.

I can't wait to see you too. But I'm trying not to think

about coming home because then it's all about university and leaving all my friends behind and I want to cry.

See you soon

Edie xxxxx

Grand Canyon, Arizona

4th September

We drove around the Grand Canyon, getting out every now and then to do these weedy fifteen minute walks to the little vantage points that were mapped out along the way. We'd scoffed all the way there that it was just a 'big hole' but it was a very awe-inspiring big hole, especially when the sun started going down and cast weird shadows on the chasms in the rock. Ooooh, am getting far too tour guidey.

We were going to find a cheap motel for the night but the only place that had any rooms was the rather swank El Tovar hotel and they only had a double room. That would be a room with one double bed.

Dylan's so not bothered. He keeps yawning and muttering about how we have to drive 300 miles to get to Las Vegas tomorrow and he needs his sleep. I mean, he could at least try and make a move on me. If he loved me. One kiss isn't too much to ask for.

Route 66, Arizona

5th September

We're in the sodding car again. I didn't sleep a wink last night and I'm feeling really cranky. To sleep next to Dylan and not be able to touch him is a surefire way to have insomnia. I could actually feel the heat from his body as he lay a foot away from me. Not sexual tension heat, just actual heat because it was so hot.

I was very bad last night. I kept pretending to be asleep and rolling over so I was pressed against him. At one stage I hooked my leg over his like I used to and buried my face in his neck so I could take subtle gulps of Dylan-scented air. I was so close I could almost taste him. I was practically inviting him to do rude things to me. Instead, he kept gently shoving me over to my side of the bed.

But I was the one who said we should break up, so I can't exactly say, 'Oh, I've changed my mind, get over here and kiss me.' If we got back together, it would have to be because Dylan showed me that he wanted to be with me. I s'pose he reckons that I'm going to university so I've saved him the trouble of a long-distance relationship before the whole inevitable drifting apart from each other.

And he's stopped driving without a T-shirt. I wonder what he'd do if I just leant over right now and ran my tongue down his neck. Oh, we'd probably crash.

Dylan's giving me weird looks now. I was probably drooling.

Las Vegas, Nevada

6th September (technically)

It's four in the morning and Dylan stormed out a few hours ago. When I asked him where he was going, he snarled, 'To get as far away from you as possible!' But then we'd just had the mother of all fights. This was a fight with Dolby sound effects, glorious technicolour and language that some people might find offensive.

When we got to Las Vegas, I was still suffering the after-effects of a sleepless night. Nevada is all desert so it's blistering hot. Again. It makes me cranky.

And even though I knew I was being a bitch I just couldn't seem to help it. First I insisted that we stay in a hotel because everything's really cheap in Las Vegas and, hell it's Las Vegas and we have loads of money left. Then I made Dylan drive along the strip three times before I chose a hotel to stay at and eventually I chose Paris Las Vegas because it had an almost full-scale replica of the Eiffel Tower in front of it and it reminded me of when we were in Paris and Dylan and

I first got together because I'm a stupid, sappy cow who never learns from her mistakes.

When we got to our room, I started griping about everything from the fluffiness of the pillows to the freebie toiletries. Part of it was about being a mardy, sleep-deprived bitch and the other part of it was that I was desperate to get a reaction out of Dylan. The Mr Nice Guy routine was getting really old. It's so obvious that he doesn't want me, doesn't love me. I think he feels sorry that he gave me a hard time and that's why he's being so bloody reasonable about everything. And I just wanted him to feel something else towards me, even if it was anger or annoyance.

When we went to the hotel's all-you-can-eat buffet (and at this point can I just say, God bless America!), I kept on whining. Even I was getting sick of the petulant tone of my voice and I was a lot closer to it than him. But at least I could tell I was getting to Dylan. He kept drumming his fingers on the table and sucking in his cheeks as I complained and criticised and made them take back my omelette because it was too runny.

Then I said that I wanted to play roulette and stalked off to the gaming rooms, avoiding the hotel staff who were dressed as gendarmes along the way. I forced Dylan to cash $500 into chips, even though he kept saying, 'Do you really think this is a good idea?' Of course, it wasn't a good idea, which was exactly why

I wanted to do it. I then lost the entire $500 in one spin of the wheel. I think I should repeat that line so the full enormity of it sinks in. I put $500 down on nineteen and lost the whole bloody lot. I actually thought I was going to have a heart attack, I could hear the blood rushing through my veins and I was going to call the whole thing off but Dylan just stood there, shaking his head slightly but still not doing anything.

'I want more money,' I growled at him.

He shook his head, his face almost impassive apart from the nostril flaring and lip tightening. 'You're not having any more money.'

'Well, I'm going to buy chips with the credit card then!' I announced.

Then Dylan wedged his hand into my armpit, hauled me off my chair and frogmarched me to the lifts. I could actually feel the tension in his fingers as he gripped me hard enough that I couldn't break free. I'd wanted to get him mad but all of a sudden it seemed like a bad idea. Like, the king and queen of bad ideas. Well, I realise that now but at the time, when we got to our room, I was still spoiling for a fight.

'How dare you molest me like that?' I screamed before he'd even finished shutting the door. 'I'm not your girlfriend any more. That is inappropriate touching!'

'Just don't,' Dylan said warningly, his voice pitched so low I could hardly hear it.

'Oh, piss off!' I snapped at him. 'You can't tell me what to do. We're not anything to each other. I could walk out of here and pick up some bloke if I wanted to and you couldn't do anything about it.'

Dylan ignored me and went to look out of the window.

'Are you listening to me?' I shrieked like some demented harpy. 'I'm going to the bar and I'm going to cop off with someone and if I bring them up here you're going to have to get out.'

Dylan turned round, his eyes flashing. 'Stop it,' he bit out.

I didn't even know what I was saying. All I knew was I was getting a reaction. Good or bad, it didn't matter.

'Oooh, I'm really scared,' I said tauntingly, and I took a step nearer to him. And then another and another, until we were nose to nose. Dylan was breathing heavily, and looking back now I can see he was on the edge. And I tipped him right over.

I held up a finger and waved it in front of his eyes. 'You're. Just. My. Ex', I said, prodding him in the chest with each word.

Something seemed to snap inside Dylan. And me. I don't know who reached for who first but suddenly we were clutching at each other and kissing. Angry kissing. His lips were mashed against mine, all teeth and tongues and bruising pressure, his hands were pinning my arms to my sides and I couldn't move. But I didn't want to.

After a few moments the whole mood of the kiss changed, became *tender*. Dylan let go of my arms and I wound them around him. He teased my lips open with his tongue and started backing me towards the bed. As I went down, with him on top of me, and started trying to pull off his shirt, Dylan came to his senses. He jack-knifed off the bed and stood there looking horrified.

'God Edie, I'm so sorry,' he breathed. 'I didn't mean it. It was a mistake.' I couldn't believe what I was hearing.

'No, it wasn't,' I protested. 'You still want me. That's OK.'

'It's not OK,' he said flatly.

I sat up and started unzipping my dress. Maybe lust even without love was better than nothing.

'What are you doing?' Dylan spluttered. 'Stop taking your clothes off!'

I tried to look alluring. 'Look, we don't have to love each other to, y'know . . .' I patted the bed.

'No, I don't know,' Dylan said with an edge to his voice. He turned and walked to the door. 'Jesus, Edie, I can't believe that you'd be happy to sleep with me when you feel like that.'

He made it sound like I was the lowest of the low. I was giving myself to him and not asking for anything back and all he could do was throw the fact that he didn't love me back in my face.

Dylan opened the door.

'Where are you going?' I cried.

'To get as far away from you as possible.'

So it's half past four in the morning and I can't sleep. And I need to sort out things with Dylan. Tell him the truth; that I still love him; that he's a part of me and I can't let him go. And I don't care that I'm wearing just a vest and my pyjama bottoms, I have to find him.

6th September (later)

I didn't have to look very far. Dylan was sitting in the hotel bar, staring morosely at his bottle of beer.

I took cautious steps towards him but he looked up and saw me before I could sit down. To his credit, he didn't ask me why I was wearing my pyjamas, he just asked if I wanted a drink and then lifted his hand to summon a waiter.

'I'll have a Diet Coke,' I muttered, not wanting to draw any attention to the fact that I was too young to drink in America and desperate to tell Dylan how I felt.

I was just wondering how to start when Dylan took a crumpled piece of paper out of his shirt pocket and placed it on the table in front of me.

'What's that?' I asked him nervously.

'Read it,' he ordered in a neutral voice.

I smoothed out the paper and read the top line: Clark County Marriage Bureau.

The words started swimming in front of me. 'Dylan, what is this?' I asked again.

'What do you think it is?' he replied in a really irritating way.

'Enough with the cryptic,' I pleaded. 'Just tell me.'

Dylan laid the piece of paper flat on the table. 'It says "marriage licence" here, and there's my name and there's your name.'

He looked at me for some reaction. I just stared at him in a really gormless way. I couldn't put all the words together as my brain had gone into serious meltdown.

Dylan sighed. 'It's a marriage licence,' he said. Then he took a swig of beer and the suspense nearly made me keel over right there. 'I'm asking you to marry me.'

We sat there in silence for a moment. I couldn't even look at the marriage licence, much less actually touch the thing. Dylan's eyes were burning into me, waiting for some kind of reaction. In the end, I pushed the piece of paper towards him with my glass.

'So do you want to get married?' Dylan asked finally.

I didn't know what cruel game he was playing now. Like my heart was his own personal Xbox.

'How can you ask me to marry you when you don't even love me?' I cried. 'It's all a big laugh to you, isn't it?'

'No, I'm . . .'

'You know, don't you?' I continued and I had to hide my face in my hands because I couldn't bear for him to look at me. 'You know that I still love you and this is some kind of sick joke isn't it? 'Cause it's not enough to make me say it, you have to make it hurt just that little bit more.'

I pushed my chair back and started to get up. I had to get away before I completely lost it which was going to be any time in the next thirty seconds, but Dylan's hand was on my arm and he pressed me back into the chair.

'No, Dylan, let me go,' I hissed.

'Listen to me!' he said urgently, giving me a tiny little shake. 'I love you. You were the one who broke us up, you were the one who found it so easy to be friends.'

'You don't love me!'

'Yes I do!' barked Dylan. 'I never stopped loving you. Even when I was acting crazy, I loved you. And I've tried to show you in a million different ways that I love you but nothing gets through to you.'

'How can you say that?' I wiped a hand across my hot face because I knew that the tears were starting to put in an appearance. 'I've given you enough signs to let you know how I feel and you just treated me like an elderly relative.'

Dylan rolled his eyes. 'I was showing you how much I cared about you!' he spluttered. 'And anyway you nearly died, you were supposed to be taking it easy.'

We sat there without speaking while I sniffed a bit and tried to get myself under control.

I tried to replay the last few weeks in my head to see if Dylan was being sincere and he'd done the über-sweetie act out of love or a potent combination of guilt, confusion and near death experience.

'So . . .'

'What . . .'

We both spoke at the same time. Dylan tried to smile. 'You go first.'

I took a deep breath. 'So when you say you love me, are you talking about, like, friendship love or *love* love?'

Dylan gently stroked the hair back from my face. 'Please don't make me say this 'cause every time I rehearse it in my head, it sounds so lame,' he pleaded.

That didn't fill me with a warm, fuzzy glow. Oh God, he was going to talk about loving friends and how friendship lasted forever and love was just a temporary thing . . .

Dylan pinched my ear. 'Ow!'

'Edie I'm just about to pour out my heart to you and you're day-dreaming,' he said.

I flinched away from his hand that was still stroking my face and folded my arms.

'Go on, then.'

'Well, first of all I wouldn't have asked you to marry me if I was talking about just friendship love,' Dylan began, leaning forward and staring intently at my left shoulder as if it was the most fascinating left shoulder in the world. 'If friendship is all you want, then I'll take it. But, really, being honest, even if it scares you, I have to tell you that we can't ever be friends. Real friends.'

I waited for the punchline, my finger tracing the edge of my glass over and over again. I looked at Dylan's hands, his thin, elegant hands, which were about thirty-seven per cent of the reason I first started crushing on him. He uses them a lot when he's talking. Like, now. They keep painting circles in the air.

I felt like I was dying.

I realised that Dylan was waiting for me to say something but all I could think about was not being friends. I'd have settled for being friends. Eventually.

'Why can't we be friends?' I heard myself say in a rusty voice.

Dylan tried to reach for me then but I flinched away and his mouth drooped at the edges. He took a deep breath. 'Because I'm so in love with you that I can't be around you if I can't touch you and kiss you and have you love me in the same way. And I know I treated you terribly and if I could do anything to take it back and make you trust me again, then I'd do it. Just tell me what I can do.'

My whole face crumpled and I slumped back in the chair. 'You don't have to do anything,' I mumbled. 'You just have to tell me that you love me.'

'Which I've just done,' Dylan pointed out. He leaned forward in his chair, pinning me there with the intent look in his eyes. 'Look, it's like when I did find Lenny and I had these stupid ideas about being part of a family and how I'd feel whole. But I realised that you're my family, Edie. I didn't have to love you, but I do. You make me feel whole.'

I rested my elbows on the table and rubbed my forehead. 'You're not my friend,' I said slowly, glancing at Dylan's tense face. 'I don't want you to be my friend either. I just want you to be the boy I love who loves me back.'

'I can do that,' Dylan said quickly. 'Sometimes I don't always show it in the right way but I've never loved anyone except you.'

I couldn't work out why I had this feeling like there was still miles we had to go. 'I only broke up with you because I didn't think you could love me and hurt me like you did. But maybe you hurt me so much because you loved me. I mean, I don't know what I mean . . .'

Dylan tilted my chin so I was looking at him. 'I have severe emotional problems,' he confessed with a wry grin. 'And I know that I should have told you what was going on but I'll never pull something like that again. You have to believe me.'

'I do, I think,' I said uncertainly. 'It's just never simple with us. Something always comes along to mess things up. And I want to be with you, I do but loving you is scary sometimes, Dylan.'

Dylan was still holding my chin but when the tears began to spill over, he slowly stroked them away with his fingertips. 'Maybe loving someone isn't meant to be simple,' he said softly. 'Maybe it is meant to be scary and strange and disquieting because then you never take what you have for granted, you know?'

I nodded and then scrabbled for a napkin so I could blow my nose.

'I'm not saying I won't ever mess up again because, hey, this is me,' he continued, taking another napkin from the table and gently patting my tear-streaked cheeks with it.

'And I'll try not to have scary hissy fits just to make you mad,' I promised, feeling a bit ashamed of the disgraceful way I'd acted in the hotel room a few hours before.

'Is that what was going on?' asked Dylan.

'Well, you were being so nice and I thought you were being so calm because I didn't matter to you any more,' I tried to explain. 'I figured that if you were angry at least you felt something towards me. Though when I say it like that, it does sound, well, pathetic.'

'OK,' said Dylan. 'To recap, I love you, you love me. In a non-friend, can't-live-without-each-other way. I'm sorry for having intimacy issues, you're sorry for acting like a demented, mad woman. And . . .'

'Oh, and the other night in the Grand Canyon, I kept mauling you because I wanted you to jump on me, tell me that you did really love me and so we could have make-up sex,' I added.

'God Edie!' Dylan groaned. 'I gave you enough signs that I still loved you. I couldn't keep my hands off you, all that nudging you when we were in the car and the bare-chested driving. And I was nice to you and brought you loads of presents to show you how much I loved you.'

'OK, can we have a reconciliatory hug now?' I mumbled and launched myself at Dylan. His arms came round me and it was only when I felt myself enveloped in Dylan's warmth and my head was resting in the crook of his shoulder that I felt like everything was going to be all right. Dylan shifted slightly and then pulled me onto his lap, his arm round my waist and kissed my neck. I twisted around so I could wind my arm round his neck.

'I do love you D,' I declared.

'I love you, Eeds,' Dylan replied.

I leant back in Dylan's arms and sipped my Diet Coke while he traced the tip of his finger along my shoulder. It was good, being quiet for a while, until a wedding party suddenly erupted into the bar. We'd been in Vegas, the wedding capital of the States, for twelve hours and this was my first sighting of a woman in a long, white dress. The groom was wandering from table to table, offering to buy drinks for everyone and Dylan's arm suddenly tightened around me.

'So you haven't answered my question,' he said in a strained voice.

'What question?' I said, turning to look at him.

Dylan reached forward and picked up the wedding licence. 'Do you want to get married?'

Oh, *that*. I loved Dylan. Despite his many and obvious faults and I couldn't imagine life without him, but getting married? That's what grown-ups did.

'Do *you* want to get married?' I offered.

'I asked first.'

I swivelled round so Dylan and I were eyeball to eyeball and I gently touched his lips with my finger. 'Oh Dylan, I do love you but I don't want to get married. I don't even know what I want for breakfast. I'm incapable of making a decision that's going to affect me for the rest of my life. It doesn't mean that I'm not flattered or that I don't love you en—'

I was going to witter on but the way that Dylan's body relaxed under me, and the look of relief on his face said it all.

'Hmmm,' I said huffily. 'I don't know why you asked me if you were dreading me saying yes.'

'It was a grand, dramatic gesture to show that I loved you,' Dylan protested, arching his eyebrow and smirking.

'Oh, I missed that smirk.' I kissed the corner of the smirk. 'If a grand, dramatic gesture was what you were after, you should have gone with jewellery.'

'Yeah, someone told me that jewellery might be a good idea,' Dylan drawled. 'You know what else says "I love you"?'

'I don't know. A speedboat? A sports car?'

Dylan tipped me off his lap, stood up and slung an arm round my shoulders. 'Why don't we go upstairs and I'll show you,' he purred, nudging me with his hip.

'Are we talking wild, passionate, crazy love or tender, girly, not before the watershed love?' I asked as Dylan manoeuvred me through the tables.

'Both kinds,' Dylan promised. 'And there's a few other kinds of love I had in mind too.'

And as we walked out of the bar and towards the lift I heard one elderly woman, clutching a Big Gulp cup full of coins, say to her companion, 'Why is that girl wearing pyjamas?'

And just as the lift doors were about to close and Dylan's mouth was descending towards mine, the other woman said, 'It's Vegas, Barbara. People here are crazy.'

* * *

We staggered down the corridor, Dylan pressed against my back, kissing my neck passionately as I fumbled with the plastic room key, rubbing it on the computerised panel next to the door.

'Hurry up,' Dylan mumbled into my neck, before nibbling his way up to my ear. I shuddered and frantically moved the key up and down until I heard the door click. We fell into the room and managed to reach the bed.

This time Dylan didn't tell me to stop taking off my clothes. This time he helped me, kissing each piece of skin as it was revealed. And then he was holding my hands as he showed me in many different ways how much he loved me. Even when I felt as if I'd lost myself completely because of the things he was doing to me, Dylan's voice telling me how much he loved me kept me safe.

Much, much later when the mid-morning sun was glaring through the windows at us as we lay in a tangle of limbs and bed sheets, I ran my hand down Dylan's chest, which was making a not-very-comfy pillow for my head.

'D, are you asleep?' I whispered.

'Sort of,' came the muffled reply.

'You know, this whole getting married thing . . .' I began carefully.

I felt Dylan tense slightly. 'What about it?' he said in a slightly nervous way.

I smiled to myself. 'You can relax, I'm not going to march you down to the Elvis chapel,' I teased as I heard his heartbeat return to normal. 'But it's a raincheck, right? You can ask me again in a few years.'

Dylan moved lazily so one of his legs wrapped around mine and his arm wound its way around my waist so I was pulled tight against him.

'I will ask you again,' he promised sleepily. 'But many years from now when we're more mature and have a regular income and I know your parents won't send a professional hitman after me.'

Los Angeles, California

14th September

The last nine days have passed in a hazy glow that has nothing to do with LA's appalling smog and something to do with Dylan. We're so love-shaped that occasionally I catch myself gazing at Dylan in a particularly slavish fashion or he calls me some silly endearment like 'poodle', which even makes *me* want to start with the gagging noises.

We spent two days in that hotel room in Las Vegas, getting reacquainted and ordering emergency rations on room service. And when we emerged, blinking into the sunlight, it was only a five hour drive to Los Angeles before we could disappear into another hotel room. We'd downgraded again and decided to honour the Beverly Laurel Motor Hotel with our custom as the coffee shop was in this film called *Swingers* that Jesse adored and we'd had strict instructions to take photos.

When we first got to LA we still had a couple of days before we needed to take back the car so we drove to Santa Monica and walked along the beach. It was good to be on the edge of America after so long spent travelling through the middle of it. And it seemed fitting somehow to feel the sea lapping against my feet as if it was washing away all the bad things that had happened.

The one dark spot on the horizon (well there were other darker spots but they could wait till we got back to England) was returning the wreck. I loved and loathed the car. It had been our home for nearly two months and like most homes it had witnessed everything that Dylan and I had experienced from loved-up bliss to abject misery and despair. Having said that, Dylan was more worried about the thousands of miles that we'd added to the clock. 'It's over twenty years old,' I pointed out as we sat in the hotel coffee shop and took pictures of each other. 'I'm amazed it never broke down.'

Dylan glared at me. Did I mention that I loved that he'd glare at me now without worrying that I wouldn't love him? 'Don't even think it! I've still got to drop it off in Silverlake and I don't want the engine to suddenly fall out on the way.'

'If you're that worried we could just phone them from the airport and tell them where the car is,' I suggested, catching Dylan's shocked expression with the camera.

'Edie!' Dylan gasped in mock outrage. 'What a thing to say! Mind you, it's an idea . . .'

He looked at me and I raised my eyebrows at him as if to say, 'Well, then?'

Dylan gave a deep sigh and muttered something about doing the decent thing before going to make the phone call. When he came back it was A-OK. 'They told me to leave the car in a car park on the UCLA campus,' he announced happily. 'They've got some student who's gonna drive it to New Mexico for them. I just have to leave the keys at the admission office.'

'They don't care about that car at all,' I mused.

We spent the last few days in LA braving the public transport system and doing some serious shopping. Though it seemed unbelievable we still had a bunch of money left between us, which meant we could spend money on tacky presents and going swing dancing in retro clubs like the Dresden and the Tiki-Ti. Dylan could wear his authentic Fifties bowling shirt that I bought him and I could wear one of my vast collection of cocktail dresses that I'd packed and never got the chance to wear.

We also got to sightsee. We did LA in three days starting with the famous handprints outside Mann's Chinese Theatre and finishing in the Coffee Bean & Tea Leaf on Sunset Boulevard where we saw one of the girls from *Glee* order a lapsang souchong.

But mostly LA was about wandering around hand in

hand and having deep, intense conversations about nothing at all. Oh, and feeding quarters into our vibrating bed but that's a whole other story.

The only thing left to do now is to go home.

Los Angeles – London

15th September

They say that you can never go home again but they are wrong. Because we're on the plane and, hijacking and engine failure notwithstanding, we'll be back in Britain in a few short hours. Dylan, rather unreasonably, has gone to sleep with his head on my shoulder and a little smile on his face, which makes him look about five.

It's funny but when we were in the States we never talked about what was going to happen when we got back, even though we knew that there were big changes ahead. The biggest change being the 200 miles of motorway, which would separate me in London from Dylan in Manchester.

'I wish we didn't have to go back,' I sniffed once we were airborne and I could relax slightly. 'I'm scared about stuff.'

Dylan put his arm round me. 'Be more specific about the "stuff" part.'

I plucked at the edge of my T-shirt. 'All of it. Going

to university, I mean, what if I don't make any friends and I can't do the work . . .'

Dylan took my hand and squeezed it. 'Edie, you aced your A-levels and, besides, you're doing French and English Lit. That's an easy degree, everyone knows that.'

'Hey,' I grumbled and stuck my tongue out at him. 'And then there's living in a hall of residence, it's like one tiny room and I won't know anyone.'

'You didn't know anyone when you came to Manchester three years ago,' Dylan pointed out. 'You'll make friends.'

'I don't know that I want to make friends,' I burst out. 'I have friends already, why am I leaving them? And why am I leaving you? What was I thinking? Dylan, what am I going to do without you?'

And then I burst into tears because Dylan was sitting next to me, holding my hand and in a day's time he'd be gone. And he wouldn't be ten minutes' walk or a phone call away. He'd be somewhere that I wasn't.

Dylan didn't say it would be all right and, for once, he didn't try to put a brave face on it. Instead he wiped a hand under his eye and I realised that he was near to crying too.

'I'm going to spend all the money that I've got left on train tickets and running up a massive phone bill,' he muttered. 'But just because you'll be in London, doesn't mean that you won't be with me.'

'I guess,' I mumbled. 'We fit, don't we?'

'We do.'

15th September (later)

By the time we got off the plane, it was getting dark and we were both a bit subdued. The plan had been that we'd go to my Auntie Margaret's house in Clapham and sleep there but when it came to it I couldn't face the millions of questions that we'd get asked and the being banished to separate rooms. Like, we hadn't had two months to boff each other's brains out!

As we walked along miles of airless grey walkways towards the underground station, I had an idea.

'Dylan, listen to me,' I said urgently. 'This is our last night before, y'know, real life and all that. Let's blow out my aunt and go and stay in a hotel. We could pretend we're still on holiday.'

Dylan glanced at me, and I tried to make my eyes go really wide so he wouldn't be able to refuse me.

'Don't do the eye thing,' he drawled. 'One more night on holiday would be great. Let's find a phone.'

Auntie Margaret was not best pleased and started squawking about needing a good night's sleep before 'you start on a course of higher education, Edith' but eventually she gave in. Dylan and I and the many bags we seemed to have accumulated then had to negotiate getting down to the station platform without a baggage trolley and before we knew it we were at Paddington Station.

'So where to now, batgirl?' Dylan asked as we stood on the pavement.

I shrugged. 'I don't know, I'm thinking of the names of hotels and all I can come up with are really expensive ones like The Ritz and The Metropolitan and The Sanderson.'

Dylan didn't seem too worried. 'I still have money. Money I got from a dad that never gave me anything else and if I want to spend it on an exorbitant, over-priced hotel room then I will. It'll be Lenny's gift to us.'

'I love you, you know that?' I said quietly. I looked up at Dylan and ruffled his hair. 'And I'm probably going to start crying again.'

Dylan put his arms round me. 'Pick a hotel, any hotel,' he chanted.

I groaned. 'OK, The Sanderson, it's meant to be really swank.'

Dylan was already picking up as many bags as he could and marching off to the taxi rank.

'Are you coming then?' he called over his shoulder.

Camden, London

16th September

That morning we woke up in a hotel room for the last time. I opened my eyes to find Dylan propping up on one elbow, watching me.

'Hey you,' I muttered sleepily.

'Hey yourself. You look like a little girl when you're asleep,' Dylan added in a husky voice.

'I'm not a little girl,' I told him with a smile. 'I'm all grown up.'

'Oh, are you?'

'Yeah, you want me to show you how grown-up I am?' I purred before rolling on top of him and biting his bottom lip. Dylan growled and held my head still while he caught my lips in a hungry kiss which left both of us breathless. And then neither of us spoke for quite a while.

A couple of hours later we were finally good to go. I'd phoned Shona to discover that her and Paul were already in Camden and arranged to meet them in an

Italian restaurant just off the High Street for lunch. Dylan and I jumped in a cab (we'd given up all thoughts of economising by now) and spent most of the journey attached to each other's lips until the driver asked us if we wanted to go back to the hotel to finish what we'd started. It was a tempting thought.

When we got to the restaurant and opened the door, I nearly had a heart attack. Paul and Shona were sitting at a table along with Poppy, Atsuko, Darby, Jesse, Jack, and Grace who jumped up the minute she saw us and threw herself at me. Only Dylan careering into the back of me saved us from toppling over.

'Oh God, I can't believe you're here,' she exclaimed. 'Your roots need doing and you've got a tan.'

'It was hot,' I said feelingly. 'And my roots do not need doing! I've gone white trash, it's the latest thing in Louisiana.'

Grace pulled me over to the table, with Dylan trailing behind laden down with bags. Everyone looked pleased to see us, but Poppy just nodded briefly in my direction and went back to intently looking at her menu. My heart sank. After everything that had happened I couldn't believe that she was still mad at me.

But then Paul was asking me what I wanted to drink and I was rummaging in the bags for the Elvis clocks and I ♥ NY T-shirts that we'd bought as presents and the moment passed.

We'd caught up on how the tour was doing and the antics of Shona and Paul's new cat and were lingering over coffee when Jesse banged on the table. 'So, come on, how was the holiday?'

Dylan and I looked at each other and grinned.

'It was OK.'

'It was all right.'

Shona snorted. 'You spend two months in the States and it was all right?' she repeated in disbelief.

I stirred my coffee. 'It's hard to know where to start.'

Dylan took a deep breath. 'The short version is that I found my dad and then I lost him again. Then we broke up but we got back together. Edie almost died but she got better. And we were going to get married but we couldn't be bothered in the end.'

Everyone gaped at us like we'd just told them that we'd become devil worshippers before Jesse shook his head. 'No, man,' he complained bitterly. 'I wanted to know where you'd been, not what you did when you got there.'

I still had to register at the hall of residence which was just down the road and the band had to sound check which was also just down the road, but, like, in the other direction. After one of those arduous sorting-things-out conversations that take half an hour, we agreed to split up but meet back at the gig venue for pre-show drinks.

There was an awkward moment when Grace insisted that she wanted to come with us and Poppy told her that she had to sound check.

'You're the guitarist,' Poppy snapped. 'Act like it!'

'Oh stop bossing me about just because you're in a bad mood,' Grace snapped back in a very un-Gracelike manner and they glared at each other with matching expressions of pissed-offness, until Jesse stepped in and said that he could sound check for Grace instead.

'So it looks like you've grown a pair since we've been away, Grace,' Dylan commented as we drove to the hall of residence.

'You mean balls?' Grace asked and my mouth hung open in shock. Grace caught my look and smirked. 'Girls have balls, they're just higher up,' she added before giggling.

'I don't know, Grace, you're all grown up,' I said to her later as I was unpacking my holiday bags and Dylan, Shona and Paul were bringing up my other bags that I'd packed before I went away.

'I don't feel all grown up,' she confessed. 'What do you think of Jack's hair, it's crap, right?'

Maybe she hadn't grown up after all.

I carried on upending my bags while Grace watched.

'What's that?' she asked as I pulled out my diary, which was looking a bit dog-eared and sweat-soaked.

'It's my diary.'

Grace looked interested. 'I didn't know you kept a diary,' she said and reached out a hand. 'Can I have a read?'

I swiped the top of her head lightly with it. 'No, it's private!' I admonished her. 'I've always kept a diary,' I added as an afterthought.

'What do you write about?' she wanted to know.

I shrugged. 'I s'pose I write about how I feel and what I've been doing and I bang on about Dylan a lot.'

Grace nodded. 'That sounds cool.'

I put the diary away in a drawer. 'It helps when I'm all messed,' I tried to explain. 'I write it down and things become clearer somehow.'

Grace was silent for a minute. 'Maybe I should start keeping a diary because my head is way messed at the moment.'

When Shona and Paul arrived they decided to drive Grace to the venue. I think it was Shona's tactful way of giving us some alone time. Dylan lounged on my tiny bed and watched while I put away my clean clothes and threw the dirty ones on the floor. What the hell – it was a system.

We walked back to Camden, holding hands, but not saying anything. To tell you the truth, the last thing I felt like doing was going to see a band. Even if it was a band with my friends in it, but it would have been rude not to.

When we got to the pub and had our names ticked off on the guest list, we found a quiet table and sat down.

Dylan lifted one of my hands and began to absentmindedly stroke the palm with the tip of his fingers.

'I can't believe that I'll be on my way back to Manchester in a few hours,' he said finally.

The minute he said it, it became real.

'I was trying not to think about that,' I muttered. 'It's going to be weird sleeping without you tonight.'

'Your bed is so small we'll have to take it in turns to sleep in it when I come to visit,' Dylan said.

'It's still going to be too big without you,' I told him, running my hand along his cheek. 'It's strange how quiet the halls are in that place.'

'You are a day early.'

I closed my eyes for a second. 'Why are we sitting here making small talk when you're going in a little while?' I cried. 'There's all these things I want to tell you and instead we're talking about how small my stupid bed is!'

'All you have to tell me is that you love me and that you'll see me in a couple of weeks,' Dylan said firmly.

'I do love you, art boy,' I said, using my favourite pet name for him. 'And thank God for long holidays.'

'And I'll be doing my Masters degree in London,' Dylan decided, perking up momentarily before slumping down again with his elbows on his knees. 'That's a whole year away though.'

'But, hey, long holidays,' I reminded him. 'So that will help.'

'I don't want you to not enjoy yourself because you think you should be with me,' Dylan said carefully. 'You're in London and there's going to be loads of exciting people and places and you should make the most of that.'

I put a finger to Dylan's lips to get him to shut up. 'Look, I'm really excited about being here and tomorrow I'll be hitching a ride on the welcome wagon,' I began. 'But right now you're here and tomorrow can just go hang itself.'

'Like I said, Eeds, we'll always be together,' Dylan murmured softly. 'Even if we ever did split up, you'd still be with me.'

'You have to stop now 'cause I will cry,' I sniffed. 'And my mascara is not tear-proof.'

The others left us alone. Like we had an invisible barrier surrounding us which had a sign that read, 'Emotional Goodbye Zone, Please Keep Out' printed on it. Even though the emotional goodbyes were temporarily paused and Dylan and I were arguing about whether bacon crisps were made with any part of an actual pig and if not could vegetarians eat them.

I looked up from examining the ingredients on a packet to see Poppy disappearing into the Ladies.

Dylan followed my gaze.

'I have to sort things out with her,' I stated decisively, standing up.

Dylan held his hands in front of him. 'Nothing to do with me,' he protested. 'I'm going to find Shona.'

Poppy was nowhere to be found so I figured I might as well have a wee before I went to look for her.

As I came out of the cubicle, Poppy was standing there with her hands on her hips in a confrontational way.

Oh dear.

I busily washed my hands and waited for her to speak. Our eyes met in the mirror.

'C'mon Poppy, don't leave it like this,' I pleaded. 'You knew about the road trip last September and you knew I was going to university.'

'But I didn't think you'd go through with it,' Poppy snarled, running a hand through her platinum curls. 'It's like the band and being with me meant nothing to you.'

'No, it's not,' I protested. 'You're like an honorary sister to me. You're my best friend, Poppy.'

'You could have stayed this summer so we could do the tour,' she said softly. 'But you left us in the lurch. Grace is completely crap on guitar.'

'Well you shouldn't have organised a tour without telling anyone,' I reminded her. 'There's you and there's Dylan and there's my parents and there's everyone else. And I was trying to juggle it all Poppy, but I can't keep all of the balls in the air at the same time.'

Poppy rolled her eyes. 'Oh God, I'm so not going to miss your convoluted metaphors.'

'So you are going to miss all the other bits of me,' I pounced.

'I'm not saying that,' she said sulkily but I turned away from the mirror 'cause you can't really have a heartfelt talk to someone's reflection and lunged at her.

'Get off me!' she yelped as I enveloped her in a bear hug.

I could smell the rose perfume she smothered herself in. It was one of my happy smells because it meant that Poppy was near. I squeezed her tighter until I felt one of her hands reach up to stroke my hair.

'I'm going to miss you,' I mumbled into her neck. 'Even if you are moody and unreasonable.'

'Hmmm and I might remember to thank you when I go up to get my MTV award,' Poppy conceded. 'Maybe.'

We came up for air. Poppy clutched my hand.

'When you phoned me I knew there was something wrong,' she suddenly announced. 'And all I could think was that I wasn't there for you. Y'know if we hadn't argued before you went away and I hadn't been such a bitch, you'd have told me what was wrong and I could have helped you sort it out.'

I bit my lip. 'I shouldn't have phoned you, it was unfair to do that to you,' I said. 'But everything had gone wrong and you were the one person I wanted to speak to.'

'But it's OK now?' she said worriedly. 'You and Dylan seem even more surgically attached than usual.'

I bumped her with my hip. 'Now, now, Missy, we'll have no talk like that,' I mock-pouted. 'And what about you and Jesse? I heard all about how he's been getting in touch with his inner lad.'

Poppy rolled her eyes. 'Oh, I can handle Jesse,' she husked. 'I'm not getting mushy,' she added. 'But you and me we're all right. And any time you want to see sense and join the band well . . . you'll have to audition.'

'You couldn't afford me,' I joked. 'My rates have gone up.'

Poppy grabbed my hand. 'C'mon, I guess Dylan's waiting for you,' she said as we walked back into the bar. 'I think he wants you all to himself this evening.'

Dylan was standing by the stage and impatiently tapping his foot as Poppy led me over.

'Right you!' she said aggressively to him. 'Take her. I don't want her any more. She's a crap snog!'

'Oh, I guess you two have made up then,' Dylan winked at me as he pulled Poppy into his arms and kissed the top of her head while she squirmed and pretended like she didn't love it.

'You two are so touchy-feely, it creeps me out,' she managed to say with mock vehemence. 'Well, I guess I'm ready for my close-up.' And with that she disappeared backstage. That girl was born to be a star.

The band had improved at least ten times since I'd last seen them. Or been in them. They were tighter, which is a muso term that means they start and finish the songs at the same time as each other and don't hit so many bum notes. Poppy was transformed when she was on stage. She was like a glitter goddess as she shimmied and swayed and brandished her guitar like it was a young man who'd done her wrong.

Atsuko was banging ten shades of hell out of her drum-kit and Darby was wiggling her hips and winking at boys in the audience but Grace was the coolest of all. Instead of moving around like the others, she stood rooted on the spot, making wonderful noises come out of her guitar. The static pose was probably because she was nervous and concentrating on the notes, but it seemed to everyone else like she really didn't give a toss about being on stage. She was a study in nonchalance as she stood with her head slightly bowed and her weight resting on her right leg, the cute little pooch of her belly sticking out the top of her jeans.

They did all the old songs and some new ones that I didn't know and were just coming to the end of the set when Poppy suddenly stepped up to the microphone.

'There's someone very special in the audience,' she announced. 'A former member of Mellowstar, in fact.'

I felt icy fingers of dread clutching at my heart as Dylan turned and arched his eyebrow at me.

'She's been touring the United States of America,' Poppy added in the peculiar Southern American accent she always used when she was making onstage pronouncements. 'But now she's back for one night only, so can you find it in your hearts to give the girl a round of applause, Miss Edie Evil!'

Dylan gave me an amused look.

'You know it was my stage name,' I hissed.

Poppy beckoned for me to get up on stage but I was too embarrassed. And besides I was wearing a really short dress and I didn't want to flash my pants.

'C'mon, Edie Evil,' Poppy shouted, reaching forward so Dylan could push me towards her outstretched hands. 'Don't be shy.'

Everyone was turning to look at me and with a resigned sigh, I let Dylan lift me on to the stage.

I gave a little curtsey as the clapping got louder and whispered to Poppy, 'I'm going to eviscerate you.'

'Edie Evil and me would like to sing a little song we wrote a long time ago,' she told the audience, putting an arm around me. 'It's called 'Welcome to Loserville' and it's about boys 'cause they break your heart and they never walk you home.'

Secretly I loved being back on stage with my best

girls and Dylan looking at me as if his heart would burst with pride while I dissed on the rest of boykind through the medium of song.

It was cool to spend five minutes of my last night with him looking at me as if he couldn't quite believe that I really was his.

And that's how I want to remember that night; Dylan looking up at me and laughing. Because after that, there were kisses that tasted salty from tears and a goodbye that took so long to say but was over way too soon.

The band had packed their gear away and driven off and Paul and Shona were in the car with the engine running waiting for Dylan as we clung to each other like he was going off to war.

'Dylan,' Shona said softly. 'We have to go now.'

He gave me one last bittersweet kiss before getting into the car.

'I'll phone you tomorrow,' he said because everything else had already been said. He wound down the window and held out his hand. I grabbed it.

'It was a great trip, D,' I called out over the sound of the engine, as Paul started to ease away from the kerb.

'It was more than a trip,' Dylan shouted. 'It was like, I don't know, this life-changing experience.'

The car started to speed up and I ran and ran until Dylan had to let go of my hand. He stuck his head out of the window so he could watch me as I waved. And even though he was on his way back to Manchester, I felt like he was standing right beside me.

'Cause we'd been on this epic voyage that had nothing to do with the miles that we'd covered or all the weird places that we'd visited. Although we'd had all these adventures and mucho angst and changed in all these unique and exciting ways, we were still together. I guess sometimes you have to go a long way to get right back to where you started.

I stood and watched the car's tail-lights until they were tiny specks that eventually faded into the night.

THE END
(really, really, really)

Author's Note

And so to the end.

And it really was the end of Edie and Dylan's story.

Though the question I get asked more than any other is a variation on the same theme: Will you write a sequel? What happened next? Do you think that Edie and Dylan are still together?

The answer is always no. No sequel. *Diary of a Crush* was always meant to be a teen series. I originally wrote it for a teen magazine after all. If I'd continued with Edie and Dylan, it would have left the teen domain and it would have had none of that wonderful drama and tears and tantrums.

But also I felt that there wasn't much left to say and that their story had been told. I liked to think of them frozen in time on a London street; Dylan with his head stuck out of a car window and Edie waving and waving and waving even when the tail-lights were a tiny glowing speck of light in the distance.

So, are they still together? I don't know. They were fictional characters who lived in my head for four years and then they left, which was another reason why I stopped writing *Diary of a Crush*. I don't think about Edie and Dylan any more but it has been lovely to hang out with them again as I got the trilogy ready for republication.

I love that people still want more; it's a huge compliment and something that every writer hopes for – that they'll create a story and characters that connect with the readers. Even though I didn't have a giddy clue of how to write fiction when I started *Diary of a Crush*, because people like me didn't get to write novels, I must have figured it out along the way.

I owe everything to *Diary of a Crush*. It taught me how to write. It got me my first publishing deal. It gained me readers that have stuck with me from the heady days of 1999. And there's a line running through the years from that afternoon at my desk at *J17* when I plotted out the first few chapters of *Diary of a Crush* to this evening at my desk in my study, with actual books that I actually wrote that people have actually bought sitting on my shelves.

Diary of a Crush changed my life. I hope in some small way, it changes yours.

(Oh, you know where I said that there will never be a sequel? Well, *Diary of a Crush* continued for over a year in *J17* after the end of this book.

Step forward Grace, who picked up the reins of

crushdom and ran with them. I'm really pleased to say that *Diary of a Grace* is now available as an e-novella from online retailers. We can even call it a sequel, if that's what you want. But that really is the end.)

SARRA MANNING

AD♥RKABLE

LOVE, HATE
WHATEVER

Jeane Smith's a blogger, a dreamer, a dare-to-dreamer, jumble sale queen, CEO of her own lifestyle brand and has half a million followers on Twitter.

Michael Lee's a star of school, stage and playing field. A golden boy in a Jack Wills hoodie.

They have nothing in common but a pair of cheating exes. So why can't they stop snogging?